CONSEQUENCES BE DAMNED

By

Ellen Grasso

This is a work of fiction. Names and incidents are the product of the author's imagination. Several of the places do not exist either. Any resemblance to persons or events is entirely coincidental.

Books also by

Ellen Grasso

LUNCH BREAK

PERCENTAGE

This book is dedicated to:

My support team, Robert P., and Carla F.

And to the caring people of the BEST FRIENDS animal sanctuary in Kanab, Utah.

PROLOGUE

Chapter 1
(Eight years ago)

The yowling of Jillian's large yellow cat woke her early that Saturday morning. He was outside her bedroom door plucking at space underneath it to alert her of his need for breakfast.
"Damn, I wish he could tell the difference between the weekdays and the weekends," Jillian cursed.
She glanced at the digital clock on her nightstand to see it was 6:00. The cat continued with his uproar as she reluctantly climbed out of bed.
"Ok Anthony, I'll get you some breakfast."
She slipped on her robe and opened the door. In the hallway, her other cat, Dante, sat. He was an old black feline that knew he would be fed eventually.
"Come on guys, let's go get some breakfast."
The two cats barreled down the steps ahead of Jillian.
When Jillian's parents purchased the home back in the fifties, it was a ranch style one. As the family grew, they added a top floor with three more bedrooms and a bathroom. The original layout of the lower level remained. The kitchen and dining room were at one end of the hall. The bathroom was located in the middle and the door across from it led to the basement. The living room and master bedroom filled the other end of the house.
The cats had already made it to the kitchen when Jillian stepped out of the living room. It broke her heart when she peeked into the master bedroom that belonged

to her mother. Buddy, her mother's Golden Retriever, was curled up on the queen size bed. The dog raised his large soft head to look at Jillian with sad mournful eyes. She went over to sit next to him.

"Hey Buddy," she said, stroking his silky red coat.

The dog thumped his tail a few times.

"You miss mom, don't you? I do too"

Nearly ten years ago, Elizabeth Cole received the horrible news of breast cancer. With treatment and the overwhelming support from her family, she beat it. The family would celebrate every April, after she had a mammogram and received a clean bill of health. This year that did not happen as the prognosis showed the cancer had returned and spread to her bones. She had been hospitalized the past three weeks while she battled the disease. Jillian spent as much time as she could with her. Before their visit ended Friday night, Elizabeth told her daughter to take some time for herself and enjoy her Saturday.

"I really wish I could bring you to visit her," Jillian said to Buddy.

"That would make her happy."

There had always been dogs in the Cole household while Jillian was growing up. Her parents loved them like children, but she turned out to be a lover of cats. Buddy had been adopted six years ago after Toby, Jillian's father's dog, had died. Elizabeth treated him like a fourth child that she liked to call "her little man". The bond between the two of them was evident as Buddy had fallen into a depression over her not being home. He spent most of his time curled up on her bed waiting for her to return.

"Come on big guy, I'll make you some pancakes for breakfast," Jillian told the unhappy canine.

Jillian had just begun to clean up her breakfast dishes when the phone rang. They still had a landline hanging from the wall in the hallway of the house.
"Hello," she greeted her caller.
"Morning Jillian, it's Meg."
"What's going on?" Jillian asked.
 She and Meg had been friends since junior high school.
"I'm afraid we can't get together today," Meg replied.
 "The electrician is coming at eleven to give me an estimate for the wiring in the new addition to my house."
"It's about time. I remember you said he cancelled on you twice last week."
"I know. The son of a bitch better make it out here today."
"Ok. Well, maybe we can call Ann to see if she wants to get together for dinner tonight," Jillian suggested.
"Let me see what the electrician says and then we can plan something."
"Good enough. Keep me posted."
"I will. Bye. Bye."
"Bye" Jillian said, before hanging up the phone.
"Well Buddy, I think I will go visit mom after I take you for a walk."

Chapter 2

Jillian never imagined that the events that would occur in the next three days would begin the downward spiral of a life that she previously loved. Late Saturday morning, she went to visit her mother at the hospital. A once vibrant woman, with fluffy golden hair and laughing brown eyes, barely had the strength to sit up in her hospital bed. The aggressive treatment they had given her caused her hair to fall out. It also gave her skin a translucent white tinge and eyes a tired glaze. An intravenous tube of saline ran from her arm to the bag hanging alongside her bed. On that morning, she had not received a treatment. Jillian had accepted her mother's weaken appearance and tried to remain strong as she approached her bed.

"Good morning mom," she said, gently taking her hand.

"Hello." Elizabeth said in almost a whisper.

"Your hand is so cold," Jillian noted, as she pulled up a chair to sit by the bed.

"I love you honey," Elizabeth suddenly said.

Something felt strange as Jillian looked down at her mother. The woman's eyes seem to roll back as tried to speak.

"Mom?"

One last breath escaped from Elizabeth's lips before she died.

"Mom? Oh my God. Mom!" Jillian wailed, gently shaking her mother's shoulder.

After receiving no response, she dashed out to the hallway and called for help. A team of nurses and a doctor ordered
Jillian to stay in the hallway before they went into Elizabeth's room. With a "Do Not Resuscitate" order in the file, they did not take extra measures to try and bring her back to life.
"I'm going to call time of death at one fifty pm," the doctor decided.
The nurse noted it before they filed back into the hall.
"She's gone, isn't she?" Jillian said to the doctor.
"I'm afraid so. I am so sorry." the doctor replied.

Chapter 3

By 6:00 that evening, Jillian had returned home alone. She poured herself a glass of wine and retreated to the back patio where she sat and cried. As the sun would not be setting for another hour, she watched the late day clouds float across the blue sky. Thoughts of her mother filled her head as the reality of her passing was slowly sinking in.

"Mom, I hope you find dad up there," she mumbled to herself.

Buddy had joined her, stretching out in the lounge chair next to her. He sensed the loss too.

"It's just you and me now pal," Jillian said.

Her thoughts wandered to her older sister, Patricia and younger brother, Josh. They had joined her at the hospital where they sat in Elizabeth's room to be at peace with her. As soon as the undertaker removed the body, they all went their separate ways to grieve. Patricia did not even offer to stay with Jillian, going back home with her husband. Josh's girlfriend, Mary, ushered him back to their place.

"I just can't believe them," Jillian sobbed, taking a sip of her wine.

She made several attempts to call her friends, Meg and Ann, but neither of them answered their phones. Jillian neglected to leave a voice mail, as it did not seem the right thing to do when somebody died.

"Well, the hell with them. Meg never even called to go anyplace tonight." Jillian thought.
She finished off her glass of wine and went into the house for a refill.

Through bleary eyes, she saw the torn pieces of several photos scattered on the kitchen floor. They were pictures of her now ex-boyfriend, Ben. They had been a couple for nearly three years. On Thursday, when he and his friends decided to take a trip to Las Vegas, Jillian had no problem with that. She trusted him, as he did her when she took trips with her friends.

The dynamic of their relationship came to an end after she called him to say her mother had died. As she topped off her glass with wine, she replayed the conversation in her mind.

"Are you going to come home?" she asked.

"Come on Jillian, me and the guys can only do this once a year," Ben whined.

He had been drinking at the hotel bar with a shapely blonde he met the night before. He tried to control the urge to laugh as she kept fondling him in certain places.

"So, you're staying in Las Vegas?" Jillian asked.

"I'll try to be home for the funeral," Ben weakly replied.

"Ok asshole forget it. I will deal with this alone. Have fun in Vegas. Oh, and when you do get back here, you better keep your sorry fucking ass off my property," Jillian warned, before clicking off her cell phone.

As soon as she got home, she tore up every picture she could find on him and threw them on the floor. Coming back to the present, Jillian took a long sip of her wine.

"Seriously, that motherfucker better stay off my property," she hissed.

Chapter 4

The Cole family held a service for Elizabeth on Tuesday of that week. The entire event was being held in one day. As Elizabeth was not a religious person, the family did not have any part of it in church. They used the funeral parlor to hold a wake for several hours in the morning. Once again, the Cole siblings distanced themselves as they arrived for the service. Patricia drove down with her husband, Al. Josh and Mary parked next to them in the lot, while Jillian arrived with Meg driving her. The family did plan to drive in the limousine together when the casket was being transported to the cemetery.

"How are you doing?" Mary asked Jillian, as they entered the room where the service would be held.

Jillian hardly heard her after she laid eyes on her mother laying in the casket. It pleased her to see many sprays of flowers from family and friends. Photos of Elizabeth had been placed on tables at one end of the alter.

"Um ok. Yeah, I'm all right," Jillian replied.

She kept walking and made her way to kneel before her mother. Bowing her head in prayer, she closed her eyes.

"Dear Lord, you took away mom's pain, now I wish you could take away mine. Keep her safe. Amen."

As she did the sign of the cross, she could feel tears welling in her eyes.

Chapter 5

Early that evening Jillian found herself once again sitting alone on the patio with a glass of wine and Buddy. The sun made orange streaks across the dusky sky before it was ready to set. Several dark clouds covered what was once blue. Jillian took several gulps of her wine as she replayed the exhausting day in her mind. The service and trip to the cemetery seem to go by in an uneventful blur. So many people loved Elizabeth Cole and stopped by to pay their respects. Afterwards, everyone went their separate ways. Jillian returned to her house, where Meg and Ann spent the afternoon with her. They sat in the kitchen picking at some of the food neighbors brought and talking.

By 3:00, they began to make their way out. Ann had pulled out of the driveway first. Meg was getting in her car.

"So long Jillian. Give me a call if you need anything," Meg said.

"I will. Thank you for everything."

"Ann is going back to work," Meg noted.

"Really? Her day is almost over."

Ann worked as a medical assistant for several doctors in Boston.

"You know how she is. That office can't run without her," Meg chuckled.

"I know."

Jillian thought about what Ann had done and started to fume a bit. The anger became full blown after she had talked to Barbie, their other friend. Barbie was unable to attend the service as she and her husband were up in Vermont. They had been notified that her husband's father was gravely ill and could pass at any time. Jillian understood and appreciated Barbie calling her several times in the last 24 hours to see how she was. The last call Jillian told her that Ann had left and gone back to work.

"I know. She called me pissed off because she was sitting in traffic trying to get into Boston," Barbie said.

"Good for her," Jillian said.

She placed a hand on Buddy's head and took another sip of wine.

Thinking about what Ann had done she thought, "Fuck, I'm sorry my mother's funeral was such an inconvenience to her."

She could feel the tears welling in her eyes and a painful crying jag coursing through her body.

"Oh Buddy," she sobbed.

The big sensitive dog rose and placed his paws on Jillian's chest. He used the moment to lick the tears from her face.

PRESENT DAY

Chapter 6

The cotton pink sky of the early morning loomed behind the building where LINCOLN MAKE CENTS had its headquarters. The first thing Jillian noticed when she pulled into the parking lot was a yellow barrier tape strung between the two large planters at the front door. A notice hung from the glass window of the door.
"What the hell?" she thought, pulling into a parking space in front of the building.
There were no other cars in the lot at that hour.
"I wonder if the two heifers are here," she thought.
The employees called their boss, Tracy Lincoln and her assistant, Tina Souza, "heifers".
At that moment, a white Mercedes pulled in next to her. It was another employee, Walter Sparks. After Jillian gathered up her purse and left her Corolla, she walked over to speak with Walter. He had rolled down his window so that they could talk.
"Morning Jillian. What's going on?" he asked.
"I don't know. I got here a few minutes ago and the front door had that yellow CAUTION tape across it."
Walter rolled up his window and got out of his car.
"I didn't see anything on the news this morning about a crime being committed here," Walter said.
"Geez, the whole Riner police department would be here, if that was the case," Jillian joked.
Riner, Massachusetts was a rural town located near the Rhode Island border. A majority of its poorly educated residents were either employed at the large

retail store in town or unemployed collecting welfare. It did have several car dealerships, a strip mall, and the large industrial park where LMC was. Riner boasted a low crime rate that the twenty police officers employed there kept under control.

Jillian and Walter turned their attention to the opposite end of the building.

"I wonder if Tracy and Tina are here?" Walter said, before taking a sip of the coffee he held.

"I'm sure they're parked over in the parking garage, if they are," Jillian assumed.

Another employee pulled into the lot and chose to park in the area that abutted the parking garage. She drove a large black Toyota Highlander.

Walter and Jillian walked down to greet her.

"Morning guys. Is the building being condemned?" she yelled through her open window.

"Morning Rosie. We don't know," Walter replied.

Rosie Tavares had been with LMC for several years. A brash woman with black hair, large body, and a lot of makeup, she generally spoke whatever was on her mind.

She managed to maintain her employment status by being sharp enough to know a lot about medical billing and bold enough to stand up to Tracy and Tina.

Walter walked over to the edge of the stairwell leading to the parking garage. Enough light fell from the rising sun to fill it. This allowed him to see that Tracy's blue Nissan Rogue and Tina's grey Lexus were parked right alongside the door leading to the stairwell.

"Well ladies, it looks like our bosses are here," Walter announced.

As they stood outside the building, Rosie plucked her cell phone from the big handbag slung over her shoulder. She dialed the number to Tracy's desk up in the office. While waiting for Tracy to pick up, she put the phone on speaker for Jillian and Walter to hear.

"Good morning Tracy. Why is the front door taped telling us to keep out?" Rosie asked.

Tracy and Tina were sitting in Tracy's large corner office. The big window behind them allowed enough light for them to see. While Tracy planted her squat, fat body in the deep leather chair behind her desk, Tina's rotund body spread out on the small love seat alongside Tracy's desk.

With the phone on "speaker", Tracy continued her call. They also continued to devour the donuts and coffee Tina had brought.

"There's a power outage in the industrial park. I think a car hit the main electrical supply. Anyway, our landlord decided to close this building for safety reasons," Tracy explained.

"Does that mean we should go home?" Rosie asked.

"No. The landlord had me sign something saying we could not sue if anyone of you gets hurt. I expect all my employees in this office by 8:00. We can sit up here and wait for the power to come back on," Tracy replied.

"And that just sounds so safe," Rosie sarcastically noted.

"Oh, we will be safe if we are all sitting in here," Tracy decided, "It's either that, or lose a day's pay."

Rosie, Walter, and Jillian exchanged looks of disgust.

 "Bitch," Jillian mouthed to her coworkers.

"How are we supposed to get inside? I am assuming the front door is locked and the elevator in the parking garage is out of order," Rosie asked.

"The stairwell door in the parking garage is open. Just climb the stairs to the third floor and you will be able to get into our office suite."

"I have Jillian and Walter here with me. We will be right up," Rosie said.

"Thank you," Tracy sarcastically said, before hanging up
her phone.

"Bite me," Rosie said, before hanging up her phone.

Tracy and Tina were already up in the office that
morning when they learned about the power outage. The
landlord of the building had called Tracy on her cell
phone. He told her that he was going to suggest anyone
working in the building stay out of it and the front door
would be cordoned off to keep the public out. The
elevators and lights were not working, and he did not
want any lawsuits if someone got injured. Tracy said she
wanted her employees to come into work regardless. It
was then he wanted her to sign some type of release
stating if any of them were hurt while being in a building
with no electricity, he was not responsible. Through the
magic of technology, she signed the e document and told
her employees they needed to report to work.

Chapter 7

Jillian, Walter, and Rosie made their way into the parking garage. They found that the door to the stairwell was unlocked when Rosie opened it. They were greeted by darkness, as the building did not have auxiliary lights in that area.

"Seriously? Who the hell can see in there?" Jillian cursed. Rosie stepped in front of them and pulled her cell phone out of her purse.

"We can use the flashlights on our phones. Come on," she said, as she clicked on the phone's flashlight function.

Jillian and Walter did the same.

"And away we go," Walter weakly joked.

The trio made their way up the six flights of stairs leading to the third floor.

"Do you think the two heifers thought of using the flashlights on their phones to crawl up to the office?" Jillian asked.

"If they already knew about the power outage, they probably used the flashlights they keep in their glove compartments," Walter said.

He did not know Tracy and Tina were in the office when the outage occurred.

"I just can't believe she didn't alert everyone with a text telling them to stay home," Rosie griped.

"I wonder how long the power will be out," Walter said.

"Well, all of us will be up there when it does come back on," Jillian predicted.

"Yeah, God forbid the employees of LMC lose a day of work due to a stinking power outage," Rosie added.

Lincoln Makes Cents was the creation of Tracy Lincoln twelve years ago. She had spent nearly twenty years working in hospitals and doctor's offices doing their medical billing. In time, she learned of agencies that specialized in doing the billing in their own facilities for private practices. Tracy, with help from her friend, Tina, decided they would like to be running such a business. They solicited their idea to several doctors in the area and set up a small office in Orion, MA. Within two years, LMC needed more employees to keep up with the billing the doctor's needed done. To accommodate them all with a workspace, she upgraded her place of business to the modern suite of offices inside the building located in Riner.

The area contained two large offices for Tracy and Tina as well as several smaller offices that housed three employees and their workstations. The receptionist had her workplace set up at the front door. This allowed her to let in visitors, as well as use the fax machine and photo copier. A wall of mailboxes surrounded the back of her desk too.

A large conference room and small kitchen ran along the back wall of the area. The only thing the office did not have was restrooms. Employees had to go out in the hall to use the ones shared by other businesses renting space. Overall, at least thirty people were employed at LMC.

Chapter 8

By eight o'clock that morning, all the employees had made it up to the sparsely lit office suite. Their unhappiness over the situation was evident when Tracy had gathered them all in her office for a quick meeting. They could not use the conference room as lack of windows made it like a dark cavern. The large window behind Tracy's desk let in enough light for everyone to see each other. She sat in her chair ready to address the group with a smug expression.

"Good morning everyone," she greeted them.

None of the employees returned her greeting. She ignored it and sat back drawing a heavy sigh.

"Well, I'm happy to see everyone made it up here safely," she said.

"How sweet," Rosie hissed under her breath.

Tracy overlooked the sarcasm.

"Do you have any updates on the situation?" Walter asked.

"I spoke to the landlord about twenty minutes ago. He has not heard anything from the utilities department in town. He did say he would keep me updated," Tracy replied.

"And are we going to be sitting in the dark doing nothing until then?" Jillian asked.

"Well, I do recommend all of you gather in the offices on this side of the building where there are windows. That will give you some light," Tracy replied.

"And, if you people need to use the bathroom, we do have a couple of flashlights in here. As you can see, the hall out there is dark," Tina said.

The employees managed to control their harsh thoughts, as Tracy concluded her meeting.

"Ok then, I really have nothing else to tell you. I will keep you posted," she said, "Why don't you people pick a well-lit office and wait."

As the people filed out of the office, Tina decided to stay with Tracy.

"So, how long are we really going to stay here without electricity?" she asked.

"Until it goes back on," Tracy replied, with a snicker.

A background of terrible living drove Tracy Lincoln to become a horrible boss. Her alcoholic parents never took the time to show her love or discipline her. As a child she took pleasure in bullying certain girls during school. In her adult life, she continued to treat people bad. She did manage to find a husband and their marriage produced two children. They turned out to be a burden to Tracy, as she was more involved with a career and filling her bank account. Her husband raised them with love, though. As soon as they reached adulthood, they began lives that did not include Tracy. This did not bother her, as LMC was her only focus. Her way of running it was to work hard and bring in the money. This is what she expected of her employees too. She did not have the skill to treat them with respect and value their service. It never occurred to her this could have been the reason the average work span of an LMC employee was eight months.

Chapter 9

Jillian shared an office with Hillary Johnson and Florence Duncan. They were fortunate enough to have a window that brought in some light. While they sat at their desks, Rosie and Walter rolled in a couple of chairs and joined them in the wait for electricity.

"Geez, Minnie picked a good week to take off," Rosie noted.

Minnie Shepard was the billing supervisor. Tracy had recently created the position after Tina began to feel overwhelmed in the duties she was expected to perform. Not only did Minnie have several clients that she did the billing for, but she was also responsible for making sure the rest of the employees were handling their accounts. Tracy expected Minnie to report to her any and all mistakes, so that she could reprimand the employee. Minnie did not possess Tracy's evil streak. She did as much as she could to correct employee errors and not bring them to Tracy's attention. The employees were aware of this and appreciated having Minnie for a supervisor. This week, though, she had gone to Hawaii to visit her sister.

"She's probably basking in the sun on some beach in Honolulu," Hillary joked.

"I told her to get Alex O'Loughlin's autograph if she spots him filming Hawaii Five O out there," Jillian said. He was one of the celebrities she had a photo of hanging behind her computer.

"You can tell she's not here, though." Florence noted,

"Tracy has been around all week making our lives miserable like in the old days."

"What did she call you in her office for on Monday?" Rosie asked.

Florence rolled her chair closer to the group of employees before she replied. They gave her their full attention.

"She had an issue about the me taking the day off for jury duty last Wednesday," Florence said, keeping her voice low.

"Don't tell me she's not going to pay you for it," Rosie said.

According to the LMC policy, an employee would not lose a day's pay if they had been summoned for jury duty.

"Well, I made the mistake of telling Tina I reported to the courthouse in Barnstable that morning. After we were processed and sat for a few hours, our services were not needed, and they let us go home," Florence explained.

"And you went home?" Jillian asked.

"Well, I did stop for lunch near the courthouse, but by the time I drove from there to Riner, it would have been close to four o'clock. Anyway, this all got back to Tracy. She expected me to come back here and work for an hour."

"Is she serious? Your commute from where you live now is almost an hour," Walter noted.

Florence resided in the small town of Carver. The commute along Route 495 to LMC in Riner was close to an hour. She was used to it, but she dreaded the summer. It was the time she had to contend with people heading to Cape Cod.

"That's what I told her. It would have been a waste of gas and time to come back to work."

"So, is she going to pay you or not?" Rosie asked.

"Wait till you hear this. When I asked her that, she told me she was going to check with a lawyer about being obligated to pay me since I was only at the courthouse for four hours," Florence replied.

"You have got to be kidding," Hillary spoke up.

"Her "lawyer request" just pissed me off, so I told her to forget about it and not to bother to pay me."

"Geez, it sounds like you should be hiring the lawyer," Walter noted.

"I have better things to do than to play into her pettiness. Besides, in another month, I am out of here," Florence announced.

"You decided to enroll in the CNA classes to be a nursing assistant?" Jillian asked.

"Yes, and I cannot wait."

The news of another employee leaving caused Jillian to think about her future. The feeling of unhappiness, while being employed at LMC, grew stronger every day.

Chapter 10

Another hour passed as the employees lingered about the office. The electricity had not been restored and Tracy did not allow them to go home.

"Hillary, why was Tracy yelling at you the other day when you were down by the copier?" Rosie asked.

Hillary thought about the incident for a moment. She had been using the copy machine when Tracy started lambasting her about a computer password situation. Most supervisors would have taken an employee in their office to reprimand, but Tracy took pleasure in being loud enough to humiliate the person for their mistake.

"She found out I used Walter's password to log in to the Harvard Pilgrim insurance site she set up."

"I don't get it. Why?" Florence asked.

"You know how she has the insurance companies set up so each of us needs our own password to get into their sites?"

"Yes," Rosie said.

"Well, my password for Harvard Pilgrim was not working. I emailed her a bunch of times about this because Minnie couldn't fix it either. I was in the middle of posting a remit and I needed to get a patient's account to post some money to. The first person I asked for their password was you Walter," Hillary explained.

"Geez, I never gave it a second thought when I gave it to you," Walter confessed.

"How did Tracy find out?" Jillian asked.

"She overheard Walter joking with Serena and Penny about it. You know their office is right next to her office?" Hillary replied.

"Oh, I am wicked sorry Hillary. If it makes you feel any better, she yelled at me too," Walter said.

"That's probably what triggered the nasty e mail all of us received regarding the use of our passwords," Rosie predicted.

"Oh yeah, I forgot about that," Jillian said.

"I did bring it to Tracy's attention I had emailed her a bunch of times needing the password fixed. Of course, she did not have a comeback remark for that," Hillary chuckled.

"So, did she fix it?" Jillian asked.

"I don't know. As soon as the electricity returns, I will check."

Chapter 11

Jillian glanced at her watch to see it was almost 11:30. The conversation lagged, as the group either played on the cell phones or dozed at their desks. Tracy did not have any updates on when power would be restored to their building.
"Do you realize we have been here almost four hours?" she said.
"Man, you would think that bitch would just let us go home and pay us for eight hours," Rosie cursed.
"It must be killing her to think she does have to pay us for not actually working," Hillary noted.
Jillian got up and paced around the office. She felt like a caged animal as she gazed out the window. A crisp fall day was happening outside. The sun shone bright as a slight breeze blew the orange and red leaves to the ground in the parking lot.
"I'm not waiting in here anymore," she decided.
"You're going to leave?" Walter asked.
He would never have planned to make such a bold move.
"Yes. She can dock my pay because I don't even know if I have enough PTO time accumulated to cover it," Jillian replied.
She pulled her purse out of her desk drawer, bid farewell to her coworkers, and walked down the hall to tell Tracy she was leaving.
"I will make note of that," Tracy said.
"Goodbye," Jillian said.

Chapter 12

Jillian pulled into her driveway around 4:00 that afternoon. She resided in a large duplex in the small town of Orion, MA. It was owned by an elderly couple called Eddie and Connie Day. They lived in the residence on the other side of it. Jillian noticed that their car was not in their driveway that ran on the other side of the house.
"They must still be at BINGO," Jillian thought.
Every Tuesday, the couple spent the afternoon at the Orion Senior Center playing BINGO.
"I guess Pulaski will be wanting a walk."
The Day's owned a small black and white mutt they called Pulaski. Jillian was dubbed the dog's "aunt" as she loved to step in and care for him when Eddie and Connie were late getting home. She had a key to their place to go inside and get the dog.

After gathering up her purchases and purse, she headed into her home. Anthony and Dante greeted her at the door like a couple of dogs. They followed her down the hall to the bedroom where she threw everything on her bed.
"Ok guys, I will feed you before I go walk Pulaski," she said.
After slipping into a pair of jeans and a sweatshirt, she piled her long red hair into a Boston Bruins baseball cap.
"Who wants to eat?" she teased the cats.
They followed her to the kitchen where she gave them their dinner.
"I'm going to walk Pulaski," she said to the cats.

Chapter 13

Pulaski did his happy dance when Jillian walked into the Day's mudroom.

"Hey guy, you want to go for a walk?"

The dog could barely contain himself and he spun in several circles.

"Ok Pulaski settle down," Jillian said, pulling his leash off the nearby hook.

She snapped it to his collar and they headed out the door.

It was crisp fall afternoons like today that made Jillian appreciate where she lived. A year after her mother died, she told her siblings she did not want to stay in the family home. It had become too expensive for a single person with minimum income to live in the town of Walwood. This caused a lot of hostility towards her. Patricia and Josh had unrealistic ideas that she should stay there to keep the residence in the family. Neither of them wanted to live there though. Jillian stuck to her plan and the house was sold. After learning the cost of living in Orion was less than Walwood, she was lucky enough to find a place to live there.

Pulaski trotted along the sidewalks of the neighborhood sniffing and peeing on anything that stood still. Jillian used the time to think about the blackout at LMC and how poorly Tracy handled the situation.

"I cannot believe that stupid bitch did not let us go home. I wonder if the power was restored by 4:00?"

Frustration began to mount as she thought about her employment at LMC.

Nearly two years ago, she had been at her third job in a large company. The amount of pressure they were laying on their employees did not match their low rate of pay. Jillian did some career research and decided a smaller company might be the path to follow. She chose Lincoln Makes Cents.

When she interviewed at LMC, Tracy came across has as one of the many hardworking women in the country looking to build a business. She offered a comfortable salary and the assurance that the work environment was like "one big happy family." It did not take Jillian long to see she had been conned. Tracy only cared about herself and filling her bank account.

A greyness filled the sky as the sun began to set. Jillian and Pulaski had walked for nearly half an hour. "Ok Pulaski let's head back. I'm sure your parents are home by now," she said.
He lifted his leg on a nearby tree before they turned around.
"Hey Pulaski, did you thank God you were a dog and not a human being today?" she joked.

Chapter 14

Eddie and Connie were putting together a pork chop dinner when Jillian dropped Pulaski off. They invited her to join them, but she declined. They thanked her for walking Pulaski, and she went back to her home.

After slipping into a pair of sweatpants and her favorite black bootie slippers, Jillian headed into the kitchen to prepare dinner. She set a large pan on the stove to boil a pot rigatoni pasta. After preparing a small salad to go with it, she poured herself a glass of wine. Her cell phone had been sitting on the kitchen table when she decided she would call Walter.

"Hello Jillian," Walter greeted her.

"Are you cooking dinner?" Jillian asked.

She sat at the table and took a sip of her wine.

"Yes. Mom felt like have American Chop Suey. I just started browning the hamburger," Walter replied.

Walter and his 80-year-old mother lived a 55 plus community in Riner. After many years as an engineer for a Fortune 500 company in Massachusetts, he did a career change at 50. Medical billing appealed to him after he became responsible for the bills his mother had been receiving. After several months of training from a small community college, they were able to get him the job at LMC. He had been there nearly seven years. He developed a thick skin, as he tolerated Tracy's harsh treatment. He also liked that the company was five minutes away from his home should his mother need anything.

"Oh, I won't keep you," Jillian said, "I just wanted to know when or if the power came back on after I left."

"You're not going to believe it, but it did, about fifteen minutes after you left," Walter replied, as he stirred the meat in the sizzling pan.

"Really? That heifer Tracy did not even have the decency to call me. I would have come back," Jillian fumed.

"I'm sure if Minnie had been there, she would have," Walter predicted.

"Well, that's a few more dollars that will be missing from my paycheck."

"You still don't have much PTO accumulated?" Walter asked.

"Ah, I actually have none. I guess I shouldn't have gone down the Cape for a week in July," Jillian corrected him.

"You know if you need any cash; I can always lend you some," Walter sweetly offered.

"Thank you, but I have managed to put away a few dollars for a rainy day."

"Good to hear."

"Well, I'll let you get back to your cooking. See you tomorrow," Jillian said.

"Yes. Bye bye," Walter said, before clicking his phone off.

Jillian could feel tears welling in her eyes. As the unhappiness over her employment situation grew, she found it hard to control her crying jags. She took a few more sips of wine and went to stir the pasta. The cats had joined her as they snuggled against her legs.

"Come on guys, you already ate. Besides, I need the bottle of wine, not you"

Chapter 15

Jillian had developed the habit of leaving to work nearly an hour before the start of her day. She used the time to sit in her car and read. She always brought along a large cup of coffee to enjoy too. Her employment at LMC allowed her to park in the lot of the Holiday Inn located at the end of the road from the office building. She liked that nobody noticed her small red Corolla among the hotel guest's cars. Occasionally, large tractor trailer trucks would be parked in the lot. They came from all over the country. Jillian never knew if the drivers were asleep in them, or if they had rented a room for the night.

That morning, Jillian decided to read the BEST FRIENDS magazine she had received in the mail. The no kill animal shelter, located far away in Utah, issued the periodical to its members. Jillian had been donating to the sanctuary for almost twenty years. As steam rose from her coffee cup, she flipped to the first page.
"Ok, what story in here is going to make me cry first?" she thought to herself.
When it came to matters of an animal's welfare, the outcome always brought Jillian to tears.

In the next thirty minutes, a story about a cat rescued from wildfires caused her to get upset. Realizing she had to go to work, she quickly wiped her eyes, reapplied some eyeliner and pulled out of the parking lot. "I thank God for my two cats," she thought to herself.

Chapter 16

When Jillian came into her office, Florence was at her desk logging in to start her day. As she issued her a greeting, she pulled off her coat to hang on the hooks behind the door.

"Good morning," Florence said.

She tried to concentrate on what she was doing to avoid Jillian's next reaction.

"Oh my God," Jillian gasped, when she laid eyes upon the top of her desk.

In one corner, papers and files haphazardly stuck out of the metal three-tier shelf she had sitting in the righthand corner.

The computer and keyboard had been placed in the center of the desk. Jillian usually kept them both to the left as it was easier for her to work that way. The last thing to be rearranged was the "live check bin". This was used to place checks that had to be posted for each client. She kept it horizontal to read each client's name on their folder. Now, all the paperwork in the folders had been placed upright to cover the client's name.

"Um, after you left yesterday, Tracy and Tina came in here to, what's your expression, "finger fuck" your paperwork," Florence explained.

Being very territorial, it angered Jillian to think that someone had touched things on her desk.

"Those heifers," she fumed, "It must have made them mad that I left, instead of waiting for the electricity to go on."

34

"Do you realize it went back on about fifteen minutes after you left?" Florence asked.

"Yes. I called Walter last night and he told me."

Jillian put her purse in the bottom drawer of the desk and flipped on her computer. She needed to bring up the clock for her to log in the time she was starting her workday.

"I'm sorry kid," Florence said.

"Did you or Hillary say anything to them when they were in here?"

"Oh no, we kept working," Florence replied, "Hillary was afraid she was going to be ravaged next."

"I guess I don't blame you two," Jillian decided.

After she clocked in, she pulled up her emails. The first one to catch her eye was one from Tracy. It was entitled, "PROTOCOL FOR LIVE CHECK BINS". She had forwarded it to the entire office. Under that email, Tracy had sent one to Jillian.

"What the hell?" Jillian hissed, when she clicked open the message.

It did not take her long to read it.

"Damn, I am not surprised."

"What's the matter?" Florence asked.

"Tracy wants to see me in her office," Jillian replied.

"She's probably going to lecture you about that stupid live check bin," Florence predicted.

"No kidding. Man, I cannot wait until Minnie comes back from vacation."

Jillian took her cup of coffee and went down to Tracy's office.

Chapter 17

Tracy's large desk filled half of her office. On top of it she had several monitors. One she used for office business; one streamed any activities going on in the front office from the cameras in the ceiling and the last screen she used to stream news and a movie if she felt like watching one. She always kept her cell phone in front of her, though she did have an office phone. Knowing that Jillian would be coming to see her shortly, she had Tina place a chair in front of the desk. This would be easier for their confrontation than Jillian sitting on the loveseat.

The door was slightly closed as Jillian tapped on it. Tracy continued to tap away on her keyboard before acknowledging her.

"You wanted to see me," Jillian said.

Tracy continued to carry on her rudeness as she finished typing the last line of her email. Jillian just sipped her coffee and waited.

"Come on in and have a seat," Tracy finally said, motioning to the chair in front of her desk.

Jillian reluctantly entered the office and sat down.

"Did you have a nice afternoon off?" Tracy said, with an edge of sarcasm.

Jillian controlled the impulse to say something bad. "Yes."

"I'm sure you heard the power was restored moments after you left?" Tracy exaggerated the situation.

Jillian knew the time frame was longer, but once again, she held her tongue.

"Oh wow, you never know," she said.

"You do know that you have no PTO hours left to cover the time you took off?" Tracy challenged, as she bobbed her head from side to side.

The gesture made her look like a fool.

"Is that what you called me in here to tell me?" Jillian asked.

"No." Tracy said, sitting back in her chair.

Jillian continued to work on the cup of coffee she brought with her, as Tracy prepared to scold her.

"Your live check bin," Tracy began, "Tina and I went through it yesterday and what a mess. I'm surprised you get everything posted that comes in for your clients."

"I have it set up my way and I do get every check posted that I receive," Jillian defended herself, "And any other work I need to do for my clients are in the folders that I keep in the stack of metal trays on my desk."

"That's another thing, those metal trays. The only thing that should be on your desk is a computer, telephone, and the live check bin. As far as folders for client's paperwork, there shouldn't be any if everything is kept up to date," Tracy stated.

She preferred a uniform set up of each workstation to make it easier for a new employee to take over after a former employee was fired or left.

"What about paperwork for claims that are being appealed or remits that have to be posted?" Jillian asked, "That's what I keep in those folders in the metal trays."

"You shouldn't have such things if you're working and resolving these things daily. Your remits should be posted, put in a batch and given to me," Tracy shot back.

"I also have aged reports Minnie hands out every Monday that we have a whole week to work on," Jillian added.

"One more thing that should be done daily and left in Minnie's mailbox, not sitting on your desk."
Jillian had to take a sip of her coffee to control the anger building in her. It was becoming difficult to listen to Tracy's unrealistic expectations of an employee's workday. Tracy merely smiled at her as she enjoyed Jillian's frustration.
"So, by the end of your shift, I will expect you to remove those metal file trays from your desk and have your live check bin arranged the way I have written in the email I sent to everyone. When Minnie returns, I will remind her that metal trays are not allowed in the workstation," Tracy said.
"Ok, I will," she mumbled.
Jillian got to her feet and headed towards the door.
With her back turned, she did not see the nasty smirk on Tracy's face.

Chapter 18

When Jillian returned to her office, Hillary and
Florence had already begun their work.
"Good morning Jillian," Hillary greeted her coworker.
"Nothing good about, my friend," Jillian sneered, as she
stood glaring at her desk.
"Florence told me you were in with Tracy."
"Oh yes, and it was not good," Jillian replied, as she now
stood before the ladies.
They had both turned their attention away from their
work to talk to her.
"Did she give you a hard time about the live check bin?"
Florence asked.
"Not only that, but she seems to have a problem with the
metal trays I have stacked on my desk too," Jillian noted.
"Yesterday, she and Tina were really going to town
picking through whatever you have in them," Hillary
said, "And really made a mess putting the stuff back."
"Well, it evidently was cause to make an issue out of it.
According to protocol, we are only supposed to have our
computer, a telephone, and the live check bin on our
desk," Jillian said.
"What are you going to do?" Florence asked.
"Get rid of them," Jillian replied.
She gathered up all the paperwork in the folders and
stepped out to the front where the shred bins were. After
depositing everything into them, she returned to the
office.

"Hmmm, who's ass should I shove these up, Tracy or Tina?" she cruelly jeered, picking up the metal trays. The ladies broke into laughter as Jillian brought them back down to the supply closet. She knew Tracy would be watching from the camera monitor in her office. Resisting the urge to flip her the finger, she noisily threw the trays in the closet and slammed the door.

Chapter 19

Jillian managed to finish the aggravating workday and make it home by 4:30 that evening. She was glad to see Mr. and Mrs. Day walking Pulaski, as she was not going to be able to. She had other plans with her good friends, Jimmy, and Barbie Edwards.
"Ok guys, I'm heading over to the Edward's house. You eat your dinner, and I will see you in a while," Jillian said to her cats.
After changing into jeans and an old torn sweatshirt, she headed into the kitchen to feed the cats. They barreled over to their pans and attacked the meal like they had not eaten in a week. Jillian slipped on her jacket, grabbed and purse and headed out to her car.
Jillian and Barbie Edwards had been friends since their junior high school days in Walwood. This long friendship took them through the angst of their teen years, to good times in their twenties and now adulthood in their thirties. Barbie married Jimmy several months after her twenty seventh birthday in May. Wedded bliss, though, did not destroy the bond she had with Jillian. They were closer than most sisters. The Edward's even chose to move out of Walwood and into Orion, after Jillian convinced them it was less expensive. They had been in their house for nearly three years when they decided to start repainting some of the rooms. Jillian had offered her services that evening to help them put a coat of lilac paint on the walls in one of the guest rooms.

Chapter 20

Jimmy let Jillian into his home, after she rang the doorbell.

"Hello Jillian," Jimmy greeted his guest.

"Hi," she said, as they walked down the long hall that led to the open area of a kitchen, breakfast nook, and living room.

It did not take long for six Siberian Husky dogs to surround Jillian with their greeting.

"Hey guys. Oh yes, so good to see you too," Jillian cooed each silver and white pet.

A chorus of howls and growls came from the excited pack.

"Ok guys, quiet! She's glad to see you too," Jimmy yelled over the noise.

The dogs simmered some, but they continued to poke at Jillian. She placed her coat and purse on one of the chairs in the breakfast nook.

"I know guys, I love you too," she continued to talk to the dogs.

Barbie was in the kitchen, where warm smells of baking pasta filled the air. A pot of sauce simmered on the stove and a large salad sat on the island in front of the stove.

Barbie had just finished stirring the sauce.

"Everything smells so good. What's in the oven?" Jillian asked.

"A baked lasagna," Barbie replied.

"And I suppose we have to paint first, before you're going to give us any?" Jillian joked.

"You betcha," Barbie teased, opening the oven door to peek at it.

The dogs had quieted down and retreated to their places in the living room.

"Can I get you a beer to keep you hydrated while we work?" Jimmy asked.

He had made his way over to the refrigerator.

"Sounds good to me," Jillian accepted.

"Can you grab one for me too?" Barbie asked.

"Sure will."

The trio took their beers and headed up to begin painting the guest room.

Chapter 21

For the past hour, they had been transforming the walls of the empty room from an ugly lime green to a crisp comforting lilac. Conversation had been sparse amongst them, as the only real sound came from Barbie's smartphone. She had pulled up the selection of music they enjoyed from the 80's. Jillian's silence stemmed from her anger about the bad day at the office she had suffered. Once again, she wondered how much longer she would stay employed there.

"Are the two of you happy in your careers?" she suddenly asked her friends.

Jimmy and Barbie were standing together painting the same wall. Jillian's question made them exchange confused looks.

"What?" Jimmy asked.

"Jimmy, do you like doing, ah, whatever it is you do, and Barbie, do you like to teach?"

Barbie put down her paintbrush and turned her attention to Jillian. She could see that her friend was serious in wanting to know how her friends felt about their jobs.

"Of course, I do," she replied, "I mean there are days the little snots drive me crazy, but all in all, I don't see myself doing anything else."

Barbie worked as a first-grade teacher to about twenty students in elementary school in Riner.

"How about it Jimmy? Are you happy?" Jillian pressed.

He did not have to think about it. He loved to do anything involving computers. His job as a technician allowed him to work from home, set his own hours and receive a salary to live a comfortable life.

"I am. Like Barbie said, there are bad days, but the good ones outweigh them," he tried to explain.

Jillian felt a twinge of envy. She wished he felt the same about working at LMC.

"What about you? Is working at LMC your dream job?" Jimmy asked, trying to lighten the situation.

Jillian smiled weakly and controlled the urge to cry. With a swallow she replied, "Oh yeah, I love it there."

At that moment, Jimmy's phone played the theme from the sitcom, WELCOME BACK KOTTER. He pulled it out of his pocket to silence it.

"Honey, I have to go down and give Apollo his medication."

He put his roller in the pan and headed out the door. Barbie placed her roller in the pan also and walked over to Jillian.

"Are you all right?" she asked her friend.

"Oh yeah, just a shitty day at the office," Jillian croaked, as she kept back her tears.

"You know, I think we have done enough up here. Let's go down and see if the lasagna is ready," Barbie decided.

"Sounds good to me," Jillian agreed.

They put the extra paint back in the can and placed the used rollers in a trash bag. Only one more wall had to be painted.

"Jimmy can finish this up tomorrow," Barbie said, turning off the light in the bedroom.

"Oh, the beauty of working from home," Jillian thought.

Chapter 22

Jillian managed to make it through the meal of lasagna, salad, and hot Italian sausage. Jimmy had filled a glass of Merlot wine for her that she greatly appreciated. The dinner conversation covered everything from world event to silly things the Huskies did all day. The topic of work was not mentioned again.

"This was so good. Thank you so much," Jillian said, as they headed down the hall to the front door.

"And thank you for helping us paint," Jimmy said.

"Are you doing another room after this one?" Jillian asked.

"We're still at odds about what color our bedroom should be," Barbie replied.

"Well, when you decide, you know I'm here to help paint that one," Jillian offered.

Jimmy flipped on the outside light and Jillian headed out to get into her car. The couple watched as she backed out of the driveway. They did not see the tears welling in Jillian's eyes. She barely remembered the ride home, as unhappy thoughts about her job made her cry harder.

Chapter 23

The next morning Tracy sat in her office reviewing the 90-day balance reports the employees left for her. This was usually a task Minnie did every Monday morning. Her being on vacation meant Tracy would handle it. The power outage the other day had delayed it getting done. Each report listed the doctor, patient, date of service and the balance due. It was the biller's responsibility to review all the accounts and enter a note on each account. These notes were a history of when the claim was received, the status of it and when it would be paid. They also needed to note if there was going to be a problem in receiving the payment.
Some accounts showed a long list of notes when this happened.

"Oh joy, let's see what our friend Walter did last week," Tracy said to herself.
She took another bite of her donut, before placing the six reports from Walter in front of her. He handled six different doctors throughout New England.
"Oh, Dr. Spence looks like it has a lot of overdue ones."
She had just pulled up the first patient, when the telephone on her desk rang. She noticed the caller id said "M. Shepard"
"Aloha Minnie," Tracy said.
She sat back in her chair and took a sip of coffee.
"Good morning Tracy," Minnie returned the greeting.
"Are you back from Hawaii already?" Tracy asked.
"Not exactly," she gingerly replied.

"Is everything all right?"

"No."

Tracy glanced at the time displayed in the corner of her computer. It read "7:25"

Minnie thought of the time difference and realized it was close to 1:25 in the morning over in the islands.

"It must be serious, considering what time it is in Honolulu," she predicted.

Minnie had been sitting in the waiting room of the hospital when she made the call. She knew it was earlier in Massachusetts and that Tracy would be at the office.

"My sister was in a car accident early this evening. Some stupid person on a cell phone rear ended her at a red light. They have her in the ICU where she's in a coma," Minnie explained.

Thinking about her sister's fight for life caused tears to cloud her eyes. She tried to control her voice as she continued her conversation with Tracy.

"I'm really sorry."

"Thank you. Um, what I need to ask you now, is for more time off," Minnie slowly said, "I want to stay here until she recovers."

Tracy realized the pain Minnie was going through, but she did not relish the fact of allowing her to take an indefinite amount of time off.

"Her husband, Nick and I are the only ones she has here. They don't have any kids and we don't have any more siblings," Minnie continued.

Tracy quickly pulled up the screen that displayed an employee's hours, as well as available PTO time. She clicked on Minnie's name to see that after using 40 hours to vacation in Hawaii, she would only have 20 hours left. She would need to begin working again to accumulate more.

"Tracy, are you still there?"

"Yes. So, how much time do you think you will need to take off?" she asked.

"Right now, I am not sure. I was thinking maybe I could request a leave of absence. I know you have a company policy for that."

"Yes, we do."

"Well, I am going to request one then," Minnie decided.

"You realize we have a protocol for that," Tracy challenged.

Minnie rolled her eyes in a fit of exasperation. The last thing she needed to deal with now, was being badgered by Tracy.

"Yes, I do," she replied, through clenched teeth.

"Well then, how about emailing me the request and I will take care of everything else?" Tracy suggested.

"I can do that. My only problem will be as to how much time I will need off. I can't predict what is going to happen to Andria," Minnie said, referring to her sister.

"LMC's policy only allows you sixty days," Tracy informed her, "If you need longer than that, we can discuss it then."

"OK, I understand."

"Well, I will be looking out for your email request. Bye."

"Goodbye" Minnie said.

Chapter 24

The phone conversation with Minnie caused Tracy to boil in anger. She needed to update Tina of the situation.

Taking her cup of coffee, she headed over to Tina's office.

"I do not fucking believe it" were the first words to come out of her mouth upon stepping inside.

Tina looked up from her computer and turned her attention to Tracy.

"What's the matter?" she asked.

Tracy had pulled up a chair to situate herself in front of Tina's desk.

"I just got off the phone with Minnie," Tracy began.

"Is she back from her trip already?"

"Oh no. She's still in Hawaii."

Tina looked at her watch and said, "Isn't it almost two in the morning over there?"

"Yes."

"So, why was she calling you?" Tina pressed.

She was confused as to where the conversation was going.

"She said her sister was hurt in a car accident. It put her in the hospital where she is now in a coma," Tracy began.

"Oh, that's too bad," Tina said.

Her haughty tone only emphasized the dislike she felt for Minnie. Her bitterness stemmed from jealously that the employees liked their billing supervisor better than her.

"Minnie wants to stay in Hawaii until she recovers."

"If she's in a coma, there is not telling how long she will be in it or if she will even survive."

"My thoughts exactly," Tracy said.

"If memory serves me, Minnie doesn't have many hours of PTO left after taking 40 of them to vacation," Tina recalled.

"That's why she is going to email me a request for a leave of absence," Tracy said, setting her cup on Tina's desk.

"Really? Are you going to approve it?"

"I'm not sure. I did remind her LMC has a protocol for taking it. You know, like it must be requested at least four weeks before it is going to be taken," Tracy replied.

"I know that."

"And the person requesting it needs to be sure the work they are responsible for has another person assigned to do it."

"Plus, they have to sit down with me so that I can be updated on everything going on with their clients," Tina added.

"I guess Minnie did not realize what needs to be done for a leave of absence. Let's have a staff meeting to update our employees."

"I'll send a company email now."

"And after the meeting, I think you and I need to do a little snooping in Minnie's office. I know she has Rosie covering her work this week, but I have a feeling there were some things that just weren't getting done," Tracy planned.

"I am always here to help you," Tina cooed with her taunting smile.

Chapter 25

Later that morning, the LMC employees gathered in the conference room for the meeting about leave of absence protocol. The small group of about 25 people sat around the long black table that filled the middle of the room. Tracy took her position at the head, with Tina on her left side. Before the start of each meeting, she passed around a sheet that had to be signed by all that attended. Bringing a notebook and pen was another meeting requirement enforced by Tracy. Jillian always took a seat at the opposite end of the table. She like to scribble rude comments when management made stupid remarks or requests.

This morning she had Walter and Rosie seated next to her. They knew about Jillian's need to express herself in her notebook, as they glanced over to see what she had written. When Tina told all of them that the meeting was about requesting a leave of absence, Jillian wrote, "I wish I could take one."
They both looked at each other and suppressed the urge to laugh.

The meeting went on for about ten more minutes, as Tracy rambled on about the protocol. She also answered a few questions the staff asked. In the end, she neglected to tell them about Minnie and what had happened to her sister.
"That's it for now," Tracy concluded the meeting.
"I will email all of you what we discussed here too," Tina added.

As the employees rose and filed out of the room, Tracy turned her attention to Tina.

"Come on Tina, lets head over to Minnie's office to see if she is going to get her leave of absence."

Chapter 26

Minnie's office was one of the smaller ones next to Tina's. Limited space allowed her to have a desk, chair, and small two drawer file cabinet inside the room. When she needed to meet with one of the employees, they had to bring a chair in from the nearby lunch alcove to sit. This is what Tina did, as Tracy took a seat behind Minnie's desk.
"All right now. I will fire up her computer here and see what is going on. Why don't you see what she has in the file cabinets?" Tracy suggested, as she turned on Minnie's computer.
While it took some time for it to load, she opened the top drawer of the desk. It only held office supplies like pens, paper clips, a tape dispenser, and a stapler. In the second drawer, she kept several hanging files filled with a folder for each of her clients. Tracy shook her head in disgust.
"I guess this is her way of keeping metal trays off her desk," she said.
Tina had placed her chair behind the file cabinet as sat down next to Tracy. When she tugged on the drawer, she realized it was locked.
"Did you see a key in her desk for this file cabinet?" she asked.
Tracy pulled open the top drawer to see a fob of small keys. She plucked it out and handed it to Tina.
"It must be one of these."

The first two keys did not fit the file lock, but the third key Tina tried did. When she rolled open the drawer, it contained four folders of different colors. They had been labeled with the name of each client Minnie was responsible for.

"That's odd, why would she keep two sets of folders on her clients?" Tina puzzled.

Tracy rolled her chair closer to the file cabinet and pulled one out. It was for Doctor Marvin Lester. After opening it, she spread the contents out on the desk.

"Oh my God," Tracy gasped, after examining the form in front of her.

It was one of the invoices LMC sent to their clients listing charges they owed for services.

"What is it?" Tina asked, moving in to have a closer look.

"Our billing invoice for Dr. Lester," she replied.

Each employee had the responsibility of listing all the services they did for a client on this sheet. Broken down into several columns, they recorded how many claims they mailed out each day, the amount of remits they posted payments from and the number of appeals they worked on.

In the miscellaneous box they were to post how long they spent on phone calls to insurance companies or patients. Tracy had developed a fee schedule for each service.

Part of Minnie's job was to fill in the fee and tally up the total due on the invoice, after she received it from one of the billers. The last week of the month, she forwarded all of them over to Tracy to review and sign off on. Then they were mailed out.

"I never knew she kept a copy of them," Tina said, looking at the sheet too.

"Me neither. What I see here though, is not the amount I signed off on. I recall the August invoice was for about $100.00 more," Tracy said.

Tina knew about her padding the invoice with extra charges if it was under a certain amount. She never realized Minnie was aware of the dishonestly too.

Chapter 27

Within the next thirty minutes, Tracy had gone through all of Minnie's folders. She used the computer program that she designed to compare what she had signed off on to what Minnie mailed to the client. Tina could see her fuming with each entry she keyed in.
"This is just unbelievable," Tracy said, sitting back in anger.
Spittle formed around her mouth as she used her thumb and index finger to remove it. Tina had been keeping a tally of the amount due being billed against what was billed on the calculator. It was close to $2000.00 the company would not receive.
"I can almost recall the heated discussion I had with Minnie after I added some things to Dr. O'Toole's invoice. She didn't think it was right to bill the client for us sending out a claim we knew would be rejected for timely filing," Tracy ranted.
"She ran a few things by me too, and I told her to bill the client after she did them," Tina said.
Tracy logged out of the program, while Tina gathered up the paperwork to return to the folders.
"What are you going to do?" Tina asked.
"Of course, we can't rebill, but I am going to take these folders," Tracy planned, "And then we are going back to my office to compose Minnie's letter of termination."

Chapter 28

        After another stress filled day at LMC, Jillian
could hardly wait to walk through the door. She could
guarantee greetings from her cats when they realized she
was home. Tonight, Dante cozied up to her first and she
scooped him up in her arms.
"You know you're my favorite," she said, giving him a
hug.
Anthony just rubbed against her leg and vocalized his
objection.
"Ok Anthony, you're my second favorite."
        Within the next hour, Jillian slipped into sweats,
fed the cats, and prepared a shrimp stir fry for dinner. She
chose to eat in the living room in front of the television.
While a rerun of LITTLE HOUSE ON THE PRAIRIE
played, she ate and drank the glass of wine she poured.
After her mother's death, she slowly grew use to this
lonely way of life. Her relationship with Ben had caused
her to develop a mistrust of getting into another one.
When people asked her why she was not married, she
would joke that Michael Landon had already been taken.
The cats had joined her in the living room but stayed
away from the Jillian's dinner.
"I'd share this with you guys, but shrimp is too expensive
to be cat food."
        The last dish had been dried by Jillian after she
finished eating. Glancing at the kitchen clock, it was only
6:30 in the evening.

"Maybe I'll get something done on that hope chest" she decided, as she headed to the basement with her cellphone.

Chapter 29

Jillian had converted the basement of her home into a workshop to refurbish furniture. It was a hobby she and her mother began many years ago after finding worn pieces at yard sales and flea markets. Most of the things they restored, they kept and used to decorate their own home. After Elizabeth's passing, Jillian devoted more time to doing this and set up an EBAY page to sell some of her items. The income had been enough at times to pay her mortgage, but not enough to make a living on.

Jillian's latest project was a hope chest she had purchased at a church fair on Labor Day weekend. She had already sanded the old finish off it and used putty to fill in a few of the deep gouges on the top of it. Tonight, she planned on putting the first coat of dark maple stain on it.

"I knew you two wouldn't stay upstairs," she said to the cats.

They had settled down in the basket of dirty laundry near the washing machine. Jillian had just opened the can of stain when her phone went off.

"Hello," she greeted her caller.

"Hey Jillian, it's Rosie."

To receive a call from a coworker after hours could only mean bad news Jillian thought. She stepped back and took a seat on the lower step in the stairwell.

"Hey Rosie, what's going on?" she slowly asked.

"I just got off the phone with Minnie."

"Is she back from her trip?"

"No. She's still in Hawaii. Her sister, Andria was in a car accident."

"Oh no, that's horrible," Jillian grimaced.

"It only gets worse. She's in a coma and Minnie plans on staying out there until she comes out of it,"

"Nobody can predict that," Jillian said.

"I know, that's why she called Tracy and asked for a leave of absence. Tracy told her to email her a written request, which she did."

"That's probably why we had that meeting this morning about LMC's protocol for doing that."

"My thoughts exactly," Rosie agreed.

"And that stupid heifer couldn't have told us what happened to Minnie," Jillian fumed.

"She was probably afraid we would want to take up a collection to send flowers or something," Rosie predicted.

"So, did Minnie get an answer on the leave of absence?"

"Not yet, but she's staying with her sister no matter what."

"Good for her," Jillian sighed.

"Anyway, I told her to keep me posted," Rosie said, "Hey, a few of us are at Canterbury's in town here having a drink. Why don't you join us?"

"No thanks, I have things to do at home," Jillian quickly declined.

"I don't know girl. It's time you got back on the horse and started dating," Rosie ribbed her friend.

"I'm doing ok without a "horse" right now. Thank you," Jillian defended herself.

"All right then, see you at work," Rosie said, hanging up the phone.

Jillian clicked her phone off and set it on the step where she was sitting. She thought about Minnie and the horrible time that she must be going through.

"Poor Minnie," she said to herself.

The cats seem to sense her sadness, as they jumped out of the laundry basket to be with her. She could feel the tears welling in her eyes.

"Is anything good ever going to happen?" she asked the cats.

Her unhappiness made her forget about the hope chest. It would not be receiving a coat of stain that evening.

Instead, a glass of wine was needed.

Chapter 30

On Monday morning Tracy sent the staff an email regarding a special meeting to be held at 9:00. She did not tell them what it was going to be about. When they all gathered in the conference room, Tina was sitting at the head of the table. She had brought a yellow legal pad and discreetly recorded remarks she overheard as the employees talked amongst themselves. Rosie, Walter, and Jillian were at the opposite end of the table, but she managed to overhear what they were saying.
"I bet this meeting is about Minnie," Rosie said.
"Did you hear from her over the weekend?" Jillian asked.
"I talked to her Saturday night," Rosie replied, "Her sister is still in a coma."
"I feel so bad for her," Walter said.
"I think I'll try to give her a call when I figure out the time difference," Jillian decided.
"I got her address out there and I sent her a bouquet of balloons to cheer her up," Rosie said.
At that moment, Tracy entered the conference room. She placed her large cup of coffee on the table, before taking her seat next to Tina.
"Good morning everyone. I know Mondays are hectic, so I will keep this short," she addressed the staff.
Jillian had her notebook poised in front of her to jot down sarcastic remarks when Tracy or Tina spoke.
"I am sure that all of you have heard about Minnie and her sister's car accident," Tracy began.

"Do you know how her sister is doing?" Walter blurted out.

"No, I haven't talked to Minnie since last week. Have any of you people talked to her?" Tracy asked.
The group remained silent. They were not aware that Tina had written on her pad "Rosie sent her balloons". She pushed it over a little for Tracy to see. They looked at each other rolling their eyes.
"At any rate, I want to update all of you that Minnie is no longer an employee for Lincoln Makes Cents. The circumstances behind her departure are really of no concern to the rest of you."
"Are you going to hire a new billing supervisor to replace her?" Florence asked.
"I have not decided yet. For the moment, anything that you would have wanted Minnie to take care of, I want you to bring to Tina," Tracy replied.
"OMG. That really sucks," Jillian scribbled on her notepad. The thought of sitting in an office alone with Tina repulsed her.
"I also do not think it is appropriate to send Minnie anything. She is no longer an employee here," Tracy added. She practically glared at Rosie when she said that. None of the people protested. They knew how nasty Tracy acted if a personal situation arose in their lives.
"If there are no more questions or concerns, we can all head back to work," Tracy said.
"I have one," Rosie spoke up, "Should I continue to handle the billing for the clients Minnie use to have?"
After discovering Minnie corrected the invoices that Tracy had padded with extra charges, she decided she would take care of the clients.
"No. Tina and I are going to handle them. Just gather up all that you have been doing the past week and leave it in my mailbox."

"Will do," Rosie said with a smile.
"Can those heifers handle it all?" Jillian wrote in her notebook.
Walter saw it and suppressed the urge to laugh.
"Any other concerns?" Tracy asked.
When there were none, she dismissed the group.

Chapter 31

Minnie and her brother-in-law, Nick spent the day at Andria's bedside reading her favorite, Danielle Steel, and praying for her to open her eyes. By eight o'clock visiting hours ended and her condition remained the same. Reluctantly, they left the room. The staff assured them, though, that they would be notified if there were any changes.

When Nick pulled into the driveway of his home that evening, Millie Lyle came running over. She was a retired schoolteacher living alone next door to him. Though she kept herself busy, she did look of for her neighbors and helped them anyway she could. She waited for Nick to park and walked over to the driver's side of the car.

"Good evening Millie," Nick said, as he got out of the car.

Minnie got out too and walked over to the two of them. They noticed Millie had an 8 x 10 FEDEX envelop in her hand.

"Good evening. How is Andria doing?" Millie asked.

"There's been no change," Nick replied.

She could read the sadness and saw the exhaustion in Nick and Minnie's eyes.

"Oh dear. I am so sorry," Millie said.

"Thank you," Minnie said.

"Well, I won't keep the two of you. I signed for this package from FEDEX for Minnie. I hope you don't mind."

“Not at all. Thank you so much,” Minnie assured her, as she took the delivery.

“Well, I’ll be on my way. If you need anything else,” Millie said, heading back to her home.

“Thank you again,” Nick said.

Minnie looked at the envelope to see that the corner address was that of LMC. She also noticed under her name on the addressee’s label, a long black mark covered the title of “BILLING SUPERVISOR”.

Chapter 32

Nick and Andria resided in a small ranch style home in Honolulu. They fell in love with the area, after their honeymoon several years ago and decided it was where they wanted to live. Despite the high cost of living on the island, they both held employment in well-paying fields. He was a senior partner in one of the largest investment companies in the country, while Andria was able to work her way up to CEO of highly rated skilled nursing facility. They were so involved in their careers, they never thought about starting a family.

The lights had already lit up the inside of the house, when Nick and Minnie walked in. It boasted an open floor plan with the kitchen, living room and dining room spread out before them. Down the hall off the living room were two bedrooms, a bathroom, and the master suite.

"Who is that letter from?" Nick asked, as he threw his car keys on the kitchen counter.

Minnie glanced at the address in the corner, as she took a seat at the island in front of the counter.

"My place of employment," she replied.

She also noticed the black mark under her name.

Nick pulled two bottles of beer out of the refrigerator and took a seat next to her. He slid one over to Minnie.

"Thanks," she said, twisting off the top.

Nick opened his beer and took a sip.

"It looks like there's more than a letter in there," he noted.

Minnie had been a little hesitant to open it, so she took a
drink of her beer.
"I know," she agreed.
It took her several more seconds, before she tore the strip
off the top to open the envelope.
	The first thing that she pulled out was a letter
from Tracy.

"Dear Minnie:
This letter serves a notice to terminate your
employment at Lincoln Makes Cents. My decision is
based on your most recent actions of non-compliance to
the company guidelines for a scheduled leave of absence
and the status of your client's workload.
Your last paycheck will be dated 9/9/2016 and your
health insurance will be cancelled on that date too.
Please complete the exit interview via fax, US mail or in
person.
Please return all items belonging to this office in person
or via a certified package to me.
Please contact me via phone or email to make
arrangements to collect your personal belongings left in
this office.

Regards,
Tracy Lincoln
President

	Minnie had to read the letter a second time.
Swallowing down half the bottle of beer, a wave of
disbelief washed over her. By her actions, Nick knew the
letter was not good news.
"What's wrong, Minnie?" he asked.
"I've been fired from LMC," she softly replied.

She handed the letter over to Nick for him to read, while she emptied the contents of the envelope. She found the exit interview and a self-addressed envelope with no postage on it. There was also information about collecting unemployment in Massachusetts. As LMC used direct deposit, only a copy of Minnie's last pay stub had been added. Tracy circled in red that she owed Minnie only twenty hours of PTO. For this, she wrote a company check.

"I really can't believe she did this to me," Minnie sighed.

"It is pretty harsh, considering what you are going through now," Nick sympathized, placing the letter on the table.

"I wondered why it took her so long to respond to my email request," Minnie said, "She must have been cooking up this little package."

"It does look like she included everything."

"She couldn't have composed this letter though. She's not that intelligent. I'm sure Tina did it and she just signed it," Minnie predicted.

"You know, my office has a pretty good legal team. If you need to, I can ask one of them if you should sue her or not," Nick lightly joked.

"Thank you. Right now, though, my only concern is Andria," Minnie replied, as she began to gather up Tracy's papers and put them back in the envelope.

Nick could see his sister-in-law was trying hard to hold back the tears. He knew that a good person like her did not deserve such treatment.

"I understand that," he said.

"I am not even going to waste money on a phone call to her. I will just send her an email saying I received her package."

"That's the way to handle it."

He gave her a smile as they clinked their beer bottles in a toast. She forced herself to smile.

"Thank you," she said.

"Minnie, you know if you need any financial help, Andria and I are here for you."

"That's sweet, but I have put away enough to pay my rent and bills for at least a year."

"I sort of figured that. Andria always jokes you have the first dollar you earned babysitting Markie Milligan," Nick recalled.

Sharing a memory about the one they loved made them smile. They finished off their beers.

"Nick, maybe this is a wake-up call to start a new chapter in my life ah, career wise," Minnie suddenly said.

"Do you mean leave the medical billing profession?"

"Exactly."

"Did you have something in mind?"

"Well, this past week visiting the nursing home Andria works at reminded me of how much fun I use to have when I volunteered at the one back home. I was in high school at the time," Minnie explained.

"You want to get into nursing?" Nick asked.

"I think I am a little too old for that but becoming a CNA might be the answer. The training period is shorter and there isn't a lot of medical things that need to be learned."

"I think Andria's place has classes for that," Nick said, "And they will set up the test for you to take to be certified in the state of Hawaii."

"Sounds perfect. Right now, though, I want to see how things turn out with Andria," Minnie decided.

"And her situation is a good example of how we should be doing what makes us happy before it is too late."

Chapter 33

One evening, after dinner that week, Jillian decided to head over to the local hardware store. After staining the hope chest with one coat of stain, she saw that a second coat would be needed. After finding what she needed, she proceeded to make her way to the register.

"Hey Jillian," Rosie greeted her.

She was pushing a cart full of Halloween decorations and several bags of bird seed.

"Hi," Jillian said.

The ladies stopped to exchange a few words till the phone went off in Rosie's purse.

"I'll let you get that. See you at work tomorrow," Jillian said.

"Ok. Bye" Rosie said, pulling the phone from her purse. She glanced at the caller id to see that the call was from Minnie.

Chapter 34

Rosie was the first person Minnie had called after witnessing her sister's passing. The hospital had allowed she and Nick to begin their bedside vigil as early as seven that morning. They held Andria's hand, talked to her, and silently prayed for her to return to them.

In the third hour of their visit, Andria's breathing had stopped, and the Lord took her to Heaven. Nick noticed it first. Panic overtook him, as he raced out the door to summon a doctor. The medical team rushed in, but Andria was already gone. Nick chose to sit with her, while Minnie retreated to a private waiting room. She sat in there crying until she mustered up the resolve to call Rosie.

"Aloha Minnie," Rosie greeted her.
She was unaware of the reason for the call.
"Hello Rosie," Minnie said, in a hollow tone.
Rosie picked up on it and slowly asked, "Is everything all right?"
"Andria passed away about half an hour ago."
"Oh my God. Minnie. Oh my God. I am so sorry."
"It just seemed so unreal. Nick and I were sitting with her and everything just stopped. They tried to revive her, but she was already gone," Minnie rambled.
Tears had started to roll down Rosie's cheeks as she listened to her friend's sad story.
"Oh honey, I wish I could be there with you," she said.
"Thank you. Thank you so much."

"Is there anything I can do for you back here?" Rosie asked.

"No, not right now. I am going to be staying in Honolulu to support Nick all I can. There's nothing for me to hurry home to anyway."

Rosie realized that Minnie no longer worked at LMC when she heard that comment.

"Yeah, Tracy informed all of us that you do not work for LMC anymore. Did you give a notice?"

"Not exactly. That stupid bitch sent me a termination letter a few days ago, with a bunch of other goodies," Minnie replied.

That revelation came as a shock to Rosie. She knew Minnie asked for a leave of absence. Assuming that Tracy had rejected it, she thought that was the reason Minnie decided to resign as billing supervisor at LMC.

"What a horrible person. She knew you were going through a bad time."

"I know. I don't mind if you tell the rest of the staff, she fired me, I did not quit. This will show them what kind of loser they work for," Minnie said.

"Do you mind if I tell the staff your sister died?" Rosie asked.

"Only if somebody asks. Right now, I have a lot of things to sort out. I will keep in touch," Minnie replied, ready to end the call.

"I understand. Please call me if you need anything done back here," Rosie reminded her friend.

"I will."

The ladies ended their call.

Chapter 35

Jillian was still standing in line at the register when Rosie approached her.
"Jillian, hold on. I need to talk to you," she said.
By the tone of her voice, Jillian knew the phone call she received had been bad news. After the ladies paid for their purchases, they stood together in front of the large store window. The sun had set and the grey before the darkness covered the parking lot. Overhead lights lit up the area for safety.
"That call I got was from Minnie," Rosie began.
'Really? Is everything all right?"
"No. Um, her sister died a few hours ago," Rosie softly replied.
"Oh God, that's horrible. She must be devastated."
"She sure sounded like it. I wish I could have been there with her."
"Me too. She is such a good person," Jillian noted.
"She's going to be staying in Honolulu with her brother for a while."
"At least she doesn't have to worry about her job," Jillian said.
"Well wait till you hear what happened regarding that."
Jillian stepped back to lean again the ledge on the window, while Rosie pulled her purse off her shoulder to set it in her carriage.
"What?"
"A couple of days ago, Minnie received a termination letter from Tracy. It sounded like she never had any

intention of granting her a leave of absence," Rosie replied.

"Son of a bitch, she is just the cruelest person I know." Jillian stated.

She began to boil with anger by Tracy's actions during the crisis Minnie was going through.

"Minnie did say she did not care if I told people what happened. She wants everyone to know what an ogre Tracy is."

Rosie glanced at the time being displayed on her cell phone as it sat in her open purse.

"Well, I got the hubby taking care of the kids. I better head on home. I will see you at work tomorrow," she said, as they headed out the door.

"Right. Bye bye," Jillian said.

Rosie drove in one direction to her house, while Jillian took off in the opposite direction. She needed to stop at the liquor store. A bottle of white zinfandel is what she needed to ease her sadness over Minnie's ordeal.

Chapter 36

A steady rain beat upon the windshield of Jillian's car the next morning. She was parked in the lot of the Holiday Inn before heading to the office. It being midweek, not even ten cars dotted the area. Across from where Jillian had parked, four long tractor trailers stood side by side. Each sporting out of state plates.
"What a good day to stay home in bed with my cats," she thought.
A swirl of steam danced from the silver cup she drank her coffee from.

As soon as she had arrived home from the hardware store the night before, she gave Minnie a call. The ladies did not talk long, but Minnie appreciated the support. The remainder of the evening, Jillian polished off a bottle of wine. It left her with a numb sick feeling that morning but it did not deter her from going to work.

She now watched as one of the tractor trailers slowly backed out. The license plate said it was from Virginia.
"Lucky bastard, heading south," Jillian mumbled.
Mixed emotions ate away at her as she thought about Minnie and Andria. She used to enjoy listening to Minnie's stories about the crazy things the two of them use to do when they were growing up. Jillian wished she had such a relationship with her sister. The two of them barely spoke after their mother died.

It also bothered Jillian that Andria had been taken at only 42 years of age. She wondered how many more things the woman wanted to pursue in her life and would never be able to. Her opportunity for a long life with Nick, having children and being with Minnie were gone.

While finishing off her coffee, two more of the tractor trailers pulled out to begin their workday. The remaining one had plates showing it was from Colorado. "That lucky bastard will be going west," she thought, "I wish I were going with him."

Chapter 37

Hillary and Florence had not arrived in the office when Jillian got there. After she flipped on the light and pulled off her coat, she started up her computer. Glancing in the doorway, she noticed Walter walking by. Carrying two piles of company mail to be sorted, he was on route to his office in the back of the suite.
"Good morning Walter," Jillian greeted him.
He stopped in the doorway to give her a greeting.
"Good morning," he said.
He noticed Jillian had not logged into any of her work sites yet.
"Wait until you see the latest company email."
"Now what does that heifer want us to do?" Jillian groaned.
"She assigned us our times to meet with Tina to discuss our work. We have to spend an hour with her, like we used to do with Minnie."
"Oh shit, I forgot about that," Jillian cursed.
"I hate to tell you, kid, but your slot is at 8:00 this morning."
"Man, she is the last person I can stomach at this hour of the morning."
"I lucked out," Walter began, "I don't have to meet with her until Friday at 1:00."
Walter and Jillian would have continued their conversation, but Tracy walking in their direction brought it to a halt.

“Is that mail sorted yet?” Tracy asked, motioning to the piles Walter held in his hands.

“I was just getting to it now,” Walter replied.

He continued on to his office, while Tracy stepped into Jillian’s office. She noticed that her computer screen was only showing the company logo desk saver. She did not allow the employees to download a personal photo.

“I suggest you open your emails as soon as possible.”

“I know, Walter told me all about the meeting,” Jillian said, as she turned to sit at her desk.

“Good.” Tracy said, before heading back to her office.

Jillian looked out the window as more rain trickled down it.

“It’s going to be a long shitty day,” she decided.

Chapter 38

At exactly 8:00, Jillian pulled a chair from the lunchroom into Tina's office. She placed it in front of Tina's desk and sat down. In her hand, she held only four pieces of paper.

"Why good morning Jillian," Tina greeted her in a taunting tone of voice.

"Good morning," Jillian said.

Tina adjusted her rotund body in the wide leather chair she was in, as she pulled out her yellow legal pad. She needed to record the things that she would be discussing with Tracy after the meeting.

"So, what do you have for me to look at?" she asked.

Jillian tried to contain the repulsion she felt being in the same room with this woman. She swallowed hard.

"Not much. I have my five clients pretty much under control," she replied, as she placed her paperwork in front of Tina.

"Goodness, it didn't look that way when you would meet with Minnie," Tina accused.

"Well, I started to take care of a lot of things after I learned she was not coming back."

"And it doesn't look like you brought your 90 day balance reports for me to review either."

"I'm still working on them."

"Well, let me see what you have here."

The paperwork contained billing problems from three of the doctors Jillian handled. Tina pulled out the first one from Dr. Mark's.

"That is a denial from Blue Cross stating the service is
non covered under the subscriber's plan. I called and
confirmed this. I wasn't sure if I should call Dr. Mark's
to tell him his patient would be receiving a large bill,"
Jillian explained.
Tina pulled up the patient's account on her computer and
reviewed exactly what was being billed. In a few quick
strokes, she removed one diagnosis and replaced it with
another.
"I want you to send an appeal to Blue Cross with the
claim I just corrected," she told Jillian.
Jillian knew she had just committed fraud, as Tina was
not certified in the state of Massachusetts to code medical
claims.
"No, I will write up the appeal, but you're going to sign
off on it and put your name on it too," she boldly warned
Tina.
"I have no problem with that," Tina shot back with a
sickening smile.
        After Tina reviewed the other two issues Jillian
brought to her, she told her to rebill them for a timely
filing denial. Then she reminded her to make sure she
billed the doctor for the service on his monthly invoice.
This angered Jillian even further, as Minnie would have
just written them off. She glanced at her watch to see that
only twenty minutes had passed.
"Well, that's all I have for you," she said, gathering up
her paperwork.
Tina noticed the time also, as she finished off her donut.
"Look Jillian, your days of fun with Minnie are over,"
Tina warned.
"I am going to get this office back to the way it was run
before she arrived. Geez, I don't know why Tracy hired
her in the first place."
Jillian stood up and placed her paperwork on the chair.
She could barely look at Tina's fat, homely face, as she

picked the chair up to return it to the lunchroom. Keeping her emotions in check, she started walking towards the door.

"I will see you next week," she simply said.

"And for longer than twenty minutes, I hope," Tina shot back.

Jillian just walked out.

Chapter 39

The workday did not end without incident for Jillian. Later in the afternoon, Tracy found the time to harass her about spending only twenty meeting with Tina, when sixty was required. Rather than calling Jillian into her office, she decided to confront her in the office Jillian shared with Hillary and Florence. The three ladies were busy at their jobs, when Tracy walked in.
"Jillian," Tracy said, standing alongside the chair where Jillian sat, "I need to speak to you."
Jillian did not appreciate Tracy standing so close to her. She did not hesitate to roll her chair to the right and turn to face the woman.
"Yes, now what is going on?" Jillian asked.
"Tina told me about your meeting this morning," Tracy began.
The other two ladies continued to work, but they were listening to the conversation.

End of the day exhaustion ate away at Jillian. The last thing she wanted to deal with was the way Tracy was going to handle the weekly meeting situation. Rather than rehash what went on between her and Tina, she simply drew a heavy sigh.
"Look Tracy, I showed her my weekly problems and did not think I needed sixty minutes for her to resolve them. We did it in twenty."
Hillary and Florence tried to concentrate on their work, but a small office made it difficult.

"Well, I reviewed your "weekly problems" too. Tina and I have decided that you are to leave copies of everything you do on them in her mailbox."
"Even the claim she recoded to resend to Blue Cross?" Jillian asked.
She hoped her coworkers heard the fraud that Tina was committing. Tracy puffed in frustration.
"Yes. Now, starting next week, you better have completed the 90 day reports for all of your clients. Those will be reviewed by Tina and bring any other billing problems you have," Tracy ordered.
Using her thumb and index finger, she wiped away the saliva that foamed around her mouth as she ranted.
"Oh, I certainly will," Jillian agreed, with an edge of sarcasm.
Tracy ended it there and stepped out of the office.
	The ladies waited a few minutes before reacting to the confrontation. They turned their attention to Jillian and tried to comfort their friend. Jillian just shook her head and held back the tears.
"Oh my God. She is such a nasty bitch," Florence hissed. Jillian tried to shrug it off and agreed.
"I know and so classless. She should have called you into her office to talk to you about Tina," Hillary added.
"Yeah, well when I do start spending sixty minutes meeting with that heifer, I will have more than coffee in the cup I bring in there with me," Jillian decided.

Chapter 40

The day finally ended, and Jillian made it home.
The rain continued to fall when she pulled her car into the
driveway. She glanced over at the window of the Day's
home to see the place lit up.
"He must be watching JUDGE JUDY and she's cooking
dinner," Jillian woefully thought.
She secretly ached for another person to share her life
with like her neighbors had.
The two cats came barreling into the kitchen when
they heard Jillian come in and close the door.
"Hi guys," she greeted her pets.
After flipping on the light, she pulled off her soaking wet
coat to drape over a chair.
"What a "fifty shades of fucked" day it was today guys."
Dante took a seat on the kitchen table, as if to listen to her
anguish, while Anthony meowed loudly for his dinner.
"I am so sick of this shit," she cursed, "Between those
idiots I work for and the nothingness living here, what's
the point?"
She wandered over to the cabinet to get the box of cat
food to feed her pets. They gathered at their bowls as she
poured.
"There you go guys."
Steaming slivers of water sprayed upon Jillian as
she washed and shampooed. The tears had begun in the
kitchen and continued as she dried herself off. After
putting on her pajamas and an oversized red robe, she
headed back into the kitchen.

"I can't even imagine what I want for dinner."
She opened the refrigerator door to discover food did not appeal to her at the moment. She pulled out a bottle of wine.
"I can't go wrong here."
	Jillian curled up on her couch with the glass of wine in hand. Turning the television on tonight was not an option. She chose to look out into the blackness of the evening as beads of rain rolled down the windowpanes.
"I never thought life would get so awful," she mumbled to herself.
The cats had joined her on the couch. The only solace they could bring was to be there.
"Working for LMC is a nightmare. Life outside of the office sucks with nobody in it or nothing to look forward to. You guys are it. You are the only reason I wake up in the morning."
Jillian finished off the glass of wine. As she headed into the kitchen for a refill, loud, hiccupping sobs racked her body.
"What can I do to make this stop?" she cried.

Chapter 41

Jillian managed to make it out of bed the next morning. She fought the numb exhausted feeling in her body to get herself ready for the workday. On her way out of the driveway, she remembered that she had not picked up her mail the night before. She pulled over to do so and threw the contents on her front seat.
"Wow, no bills," she thought.
The big envelope had BEST FRIENDS address in the corner, while the other piece of mail was advertising for a new dentist in town.

Only a few cars were parked in the lot of the Holiday Inn when Jillian arrived there twenty minutes later.
Once again, she chose to park across from the area where six tractor trailers were. They belonged to drivers from several different states. After rolling down her window, she inhaled the cool morning air and took a sip of her coffee.
This action did little to expel the anxiety that began to build again. She did not want to face another day at LMC. Taking a few deep breaths, she focused on the trucks in front of her.
"Where are you going?" she silently asked.

Chapter 42

Albert LaPlante had been an over-the-road trucker for nearly twenty years. At the moment he owned a Kenworth T800 Day Cab Truck that he used to haul pet products for Youngblood Pet Supplies. He would begin his route out of Cedar City, Utah on a Monday and usually ended it in Riner, Massachusetts on Thursday. The trip covered several states where he left products for numerous pet supply stores. As the truck did not have a sleeper compartment, he mapped out inexpensive hotels along the way to stay overnight at.

On that particular morning, he had been retrieving his HOURS OF SERVICE journal from the glove compartment of his truck. He decided he would update it, while enjoying the continental breakfast the hotel offered. Upon walking passed Jillian's car, he noticed her slumped against the steering wheel. With the window open, he could hear her loud, wailing sobs.

"Miss, are you, all right?" Albert asked, stopping alongside her.

She sensed a person standing outside the vehicle and sat back. Through eyes clouded by tears, she saw the figure of an older man, with soft blue eyes and balding head. He looked deeply concerned.

"Is there anything I can do for you?" he asked.

Albert had two daughters and a granddaughter. He knew how emotional a woman could be, but he read pain in Jillian's moist green eyes. He also noted the disarray of the long auburn braid that ran down her back.

"Ah, n-no. I'm ok," Jillian stammered.

"Are you sure? Nobody hurt you, did they?"

"No. Nobody touched me," Jillian replied, slightly embarrassed by the concern.
She grabbed a tissue from the box on the passenger's seat and wiped her face and nose.
Albert felt like there was more he could do for this person.
"You ah, you look like you need someone to talk to," he noted.
"I'll be ok. Thank you," Jillian shakily assured him.
"I'm on my way back into the hotel. I was a guest here. Why don't you join me for the continental breakfast they serve?" Albert offered.
Jillian gave Albert another look and decided to trust him.
 "Ah, ok. I think I will. By the way, my name is Jillian."
"I'm Albert LaPlante."
Jillian rolled up her window and got out of her car.

Chapter 43

All her life, Jillian had been warned to be cautious of strangers. When she sat down to share breakfast with Albert, the warning did not seem to apply. He seemed genuine in his concern for her unhappiness. All he wanted to do was share a meal and talk.

Jillian sat down to large cup of coffee and blueberry muffin, while Albert chose scrambled eggs, toast, bacon, a muffin, and a glass of orange juice. With the exception of another guest seated in the corner reading a newspaper, they were the only people in the dining room.

"Is that all you're having to eat?" Albert asked.

"I'm not much of a breakfast person," Jillian confessed, "But it looks like you are."

"I like to be full, before I hit the road," Albert said, taking a heaping forkful of eggs.

"No coffee though?" Jillian asked.

"The Mormon religion does not allow it," Albert replied.

"I remember," Jillian suddenly said.

Albert washed the eggs down with some orange juice.

"I don't understand. You know about the Mormon religion?"

Jillian suddenly blurted out, "I had a crush on Donny Osmond. It made me research the Mormon religion and I remember he could not drink coffee or Coke."

The revelation caused Albert to chuckle.

"My girls had a crush on him too. We live in Utah, but we never met him."

Continuing to work on the meals in front of them, Jillian never gave it a second thought that she might arrive late to work.

"Do you own that big truck out there with the Utah license plates on it?" she asked.

"Yeah. I do deliveries for a pet supply company located in Cedar City, Utah," Albert replied, before finishing off his eggs.

"Geez, that must be a great job. Seeing the country, not confined to a cubicle and I am sure you make a good salary," Jillian predicted.

"I have to confess; I really like it. I've been at it for over twenty years. What do you do for a living?"

The reply nearly stuck in Jillian's throat. She needed some coffee to get the answer out.

"Medical billing."

"I see."

Jillian seem to have no control over the rant that exploded from her mouth next.

"And I hate it. For eight hours a day, I sit at a computer doing things I could really care less about, dealing with things that aggravate the hell out of me and working for one of the most horrible people on this planet!"

She started to tremble a little as she continued her meltdown. Albert sat back and listened. He sensed Jillian needed this time to unload.

"I would walk out in a second, but it's just me and I need a paycheck. I need those medical benefits too so that I don't get fined at tax time, thanks to our lousy politicians."

The tone of her voice seem to grow higher. The guest reading his newspaper did his best to ignore her.

She tipped her head back and took a few deep breaths.

Chapter 44

Albert laid his hand on Jillian's arm and looked her in the eye. She slowly collected her out of control emotions.
"Did that feel better?" he gently asked.
With another deep breath, Jillian managed to control her tears. She gave Albert a weak smile.
"Yes. I'm sorry. It's just that, oh hell, I don't know. I don't care. I wish I knew how to handle this mixed up feeling," Jillian replied.
Albert sat back to appraise the emotions his new friend was experiencing. It reminded him of his daughter, Joyce. Several years ago, she had contemplated suicide when she felt her life had no purpose. His family and their faith rallied her through the ordeal. She became a better person after she realized what she wanted and what would bring her happiness.
He instantly knew Jillian was going through the same thing.
"Have you ever thought about what you really want to do with your life?" he asked.
The question stunned Jillian. She gave it some thought and the answer she gave Albert surprised even her.
"Yes. As stupid as it sounds, I made the mistake of staying in a public high school to take all those boring courses they have to prepare you to work in the business world. What I really wanted to do was go to the agricultural school that was in my hometown."

"I cannot imagine where this is leading," Albert thought to himself.

"The courses they offered prepared you for a career with animals, plants or the environment."

"I see."

"But no, I played it safe, stayed with my friends in public high school and began a depressing career path."

Albert digested the account Jillian gave him of what she thought was a horrible past. He tried to understand why she did not try to correct it as time went on.

"Jillian, if you don't mind me asking, how old are you?"

The question did not offend Jillian, as she felt at ease with Albert.

"I just turned thirty two in July," she replied.

"For starters, I imagined you to be several years younger," Albert began.

"Thank you."

"And upon hearing that, your life is not over. From what I can tell, you only have "you" to answer to."

"I don't understand," Jillian said.

"At this point in your life, you should be looking for ways to make it happy and satisfying. If taking care of animals or the environment can do that, there are plenty of opportunities out there for it to happen."

"I know. I think about it all the time, but then I retreat to my safety zone and do nothing about it," Jillian confessed.

"Kid, it is time you say, "Consequences be damned" and start making those changes," Albert encouraged her, "I guarantee it will wipe away your unhappiness."

Jillian marveled at her new friend's words, as they began to sink in. He completely resolved the problem she had been suffering through for many years. It really was time to make a change in her life.

Chapter 45

Albert glanced at his watch before finishing off his toast.

"You know Jillian, I have really enjoyed this breakfast with you, but I have to head out. My last delivery has to be made by nine if I want to get on the road before noon."

"I enjoyed it too," she said, as she opened her purse to pull out her car keys.

Sitting inside it, she noticed the donation she had to mail to the BEST FRIENDS animal sanctuary in Utah.

"That's it," she whispered.

"What?" Albert asked.

"Albert, can you travel with a passenger in your truck that isn't an employee of Youngblood Pet Supplies?" she asked.

"Yes. I own the truck. I take the wife with me sometimes," Albert replied.

"Well, if it's not a problem, I would like to go back to Utah with you. When we get there, I am going to visit the BEST FRIENDS animal sanctuary. I know they need volunteers and maybe I could get a job there too," Jillian planned.

"Are you serious?" Albert pressed.

"More than you can imagine. I won't be a problem."

Albert thought about the offer for a moment. It did not take him long to decide that a trip out West might help his new friend.

"Ok. I'll let you ride along with me."

The prospect of a new adventure suddenly made Jillian feel like a child on Christmas morning.

"I just have to make two phone calls and we can hit the road," she said.

"I need to make a call too and use the restroom. Meet me out at my truck when you finish," Albert planned.

"Ah, I think I will use the ladies' room too," Jillian decided.

She had consumed three cups of coffee.

Chapter 46

Albert retreated out to his truck and climbed into the driver's seat. After pulling out his phone, he called his wife, Emma.
Good morning Em. Did I wake you?" Albert began.
The two hour time difference made it close to six in the morning back in Utah, but Emma had been awake for nearly an hour. She was having a glass of milk and toast in the kitchen.
"Oh no sweetie. You know the Shriver's barking dogs have me up at five," she chuckled.
"I know. Hey, I'm on my way back home and I um, wanted to tell you about my ah, passenger," Albert gingerly explained to his wife.
"Ok dear, who is down on their luck now?" Emma asked. She knew what a kind heart her husband possessed and his weakness for helping everyone. She had learned to accept it over the forty years of their marriage.
"It's a young woman I came across this morning crying in her car. She was parked in the lot of the hotel I stayed at last night in Massachusetts."
"Oh dear."
"The poor kid was hysterical. After she calmed some, I invited her to breakfast, and we talked."
"And what made you decide traveling to out here to Utah would make her happy?" Emma asked.
"She sort of made the decision when she mentioned the BEST FRIEND sanctuary and a desire to help animals."

"I'm sure there is more to her situation that influenced your decision to help her."

"Well, she did kind of remind me of Joyce and the rough patch she was going through a few years ago," Albert confessed.

Comparing Jillian's situation to Joyce's made Emma realize how serious it was.

"I understand, Al. You bring that woman back here and we will do all we can to help her," Emma decided.

"I knew you would feel that way. We will be heading out after I make my stop at the pet store in Riner. I will give you a call when we reach Lewisburg, Pennsylvania tonight," Albert said.

"I will be waiting. No dozing on the drive," Emma warned.

Chapter 47

Jillian made her two phone calls in the ladies room after she finished going. The first one was to LMC. The protocol for calling out was to speak to Tina. On the second ring, she answered the telephone.

"Good morning, Lincoln Makes Cents. How can I help you?"

"Tina, it's Jillian. I don't have a lot of time. I just wanted to call and say um, I need a "leave of absence."" A family matter came up I have to take care of right away,"

She bite her lip to control the urge to laugh in Tina's ear.

"Leave of absence? What's going on? Why?"

"That's really none of your business. Wait, I will email my request, so you have it in writing."

"Jillian, what is going on?" Tina demanded.

Jillian did not want to spend another minute on the phone.

"Gee, I hope Tracy doesn't terminate me. Bye Tina," she said, before ending her call.

She let out a sigh of happiness. It was already beginning to feel good making changes in her life.

The next call Jillian made was to the Edward's house. She knew Barbie was already at work, so she spoke to Jimmy. After noting she did not have a long to talk, she asked if he and Barbie could pick her car up at the Holiday Inn lot and leave it at her house. She also mentioned her cats and asked if they would feed them. He agreed to help her out any way he could.

"Thank you so much. I will call Barbie tonight," Jillian said.
She hung up the call and headed out to Albert's truck.

Chapter 48

As soon as Tina hung up her call from Jillian, she headed next door into Tracy's office. She planted herself on the loveseat just bursting to tell Tracy about the call. Tracy had been streaming the early morning news on one of her monitors. After lowering the volume, she turned her attention to Tina.

"You are not going to believe the phone call I just received," Tina exclaimed.

"Was it from an employee or client?" Tracy asked.

"It was from your favorite employee, Jillian Cole," Tina teased.

"Oh God, now what is bothering her?" Tracy groaned.

"She told me she needs a leave of absence to take care of a family matter."

"Shit, if I hear that term again, I am going to scream," Tracy decided.

"She said she was going to email you a request. Have you received anything yet?" Tina asked.

Tracy clicked on the site that contained her emails. None of them were from Jillian.

"Nothing yet," she replied.

"Well, she did add a little sarcasm to our conversation," Tina prattled on, "She said, "Gee, I hope she doesn't terminate me." Can you imagine?"

Tina's revelation quickly triggered a spark of anger in Tracy. She pounded her open hand on the desk.

"That nasty bitch. You know, the moment I receive that email, I am simply going to ignore it," Tracy decided.

"Really?" Tina asked, surprised.

"Yes. I want to see if she has the balls to call "me" and ask for her "leave of absence." Boy, will she get an earful."

"I think she would have called you directly this morning, if she did."

"I wonder if she called Rosie or Walter. I know they stay in touch when they are out of the office," Tracy said.

"I believe they are here already. Do you want me to go in and question them?" Tina asked.

"No, I think I want to see what they have to say," Tracy decided, getting to her feet.

Tina rose too and the ladies headed out of the office.

"I will keep you posted if I receive any more calls," Tina said.

Chapter 49

Walter, Rosie and another employee, Melinda
Grant shared the first office on the right upon entering the
billing suite. Walter and Melinda were engaged in their
work responsibilities, while Rosie took a time out to
answer the text message that had pinged on her cell
phone. She had just finished when Tracy walked into the
office.
"Rosie, I hope that was a family emergency," Tracy said,
seeing her slip the phone back into her purse.
The LMC policy on cell phone use was that it could be
only used for an emergency. If Tracy or Tina caught
anyone using it otherwise, they would be written up or
terminated.
"I was my daughter's school. They were confirming the
doctor appointment she has next week."
Tracy placed herself in the center of the office to address
the three people in it.
"I see. Um, have any of you gotten any texts or call from
Jillian today?" she asked.
Walter, Melinda, and Rosie turned their attention to
Tracy.
"No," Walter replied.
"Not me," Rosie said.
"Me neither," Melinda chimed in.
"Is there something wrong?" Walter asked.
"She called Tina this morning to request a leave of
absence for a family matter. I thought she might have told
you something more," Tracy replied.

"No. Nothing from her," Rosie reiterated.

"Well, I want to know if you do hear from her, ok?" Tracy said, almost in a threatening tone.

"Sure, we will," Walter lied.

The moment Tracy left the office, Rosie pulled her phone out. She quickly shot off a text to Jillian asking her if everything was all right. Walter snuck his phone out of his desk drawer and sent Jillian the same type of message.

"Geez Rosie, I hope nothing serious has happened to our friend," Walter said.

"I know. She's a tough kid though. I don't think we have to worry," Rosie said, with a little apprehension.

Chapter 50

Jillian accompanied Albert on his last delivery to Happy Dog Grooming in Riner. As he made his way down Route 495 to pick up I-90W, she took in the view around her and watched the traffic below. It was an odd sensation, like a carnival ride, to be moving so high above traffic.
In the few hours that they drove, she had witnessed all kinds of odd things people did while driving in their cars. One lady was even brushing her teeth and gargling.
"Geez Albert, I bet you have seen everything riding high in this truck," she noted.
Albert chuckled, as he knew her observation to be true.
"I certainly have. You wouldn't believe how many people drive without their pants on," he joked.
"What? You've got to be kidding."
"And to this day, I can never understand why they do," Albert continued.
He only brought more laughter to Jillian.
"If that really happens, I don't want to imagine what they do if a state trooper pulls them over," Jillian said,
"I'm sure that's some kind of driving violation too."

Chapter 51

The drive took Albert and Jillian through Massachusetts, a small portion on New York and into Pennsylvania. Adhering to the amount of time Albert could drive before needing to record a sixty minute break, their first stop along the way was in Wilkes-Barre, PA. He pulled his rig into the lot of the Wyoming Valley Mall.

"I usually like to stop here and have me some Chinese food for lunch at the Royal House Buffet," Albert told Jillian, as he parked the truck.

Along the drive, she had been thinking about where they could stop for her to purchase a few things, like changes of clothes and toiletries. She could hardly believe her luck when he pulled into a mall.

"Um, do you mind if I shop instead? I really need to buy some things if we are going to be on the road for a few days," she asked.

"I guess you're right about that," Albert agreed.

"I promise I will keep it under four suitcases," Jillian joked.

He smiled and asked her if she would like him to buy her anything to eat.

"No thank you. I'm sure I can find something quick to eat in the mall."

"You might want to pick up a heavy coat, with gloves and a hat. I'm not sure how cold the weather is going to be as we get closer to Utah," Albert suggested.

Jillian had been dressed in lighter clothing, her sneakers, and a denim jacket.

"I'll do that."

They both climbed out of the truck.

"Ok kid, try to be back here in about an hour."

Jillian was standing by the passenger side of the truck when Albert joined her sixty minutes later. A long black duffle bag was laying at her feet. She had purchased it to put all the items she bought into it.

"Hope you weren't waiting long," Albert said.

He had a bag of food in his hand.

"I just got here about five minutes ago."

He noticed the new piece of luggage Jillian had.

"Well, at least it isn't four suitcases," he teased.

"It could have been. Man, I haven't been mall shopping in ages," Jillian confessed.

"I always heard "retail therapy" is something you ladies like," Albert said, as handed Jillian the bag he was holding.

"I picked us up some appetizers to eat on the road," he said.

"Geez, I forgot to get something. Thank you."

Albert picked up the duffle bag to place in the truck.

"Get on in and we can head out, he said.

After settling into the cab, they headed for the hotel in Lewisburg, Pennsylvania.

Chapter 52

Several hours later, they arrived at the Holiday Inn Express in Lewisburg, PA. Albert assured Jillian the rooms were clean and affordable. After hours of driving, she only cared about a hot shower and warm bed.
"I am so tired; I could have slept in your truck," Jillian said, as they entered the lobby of the hotel.
Albert was a frequent guest of the hotel and knew most of the employees.
"Evening Roger. Is it a slow night?" he addressed the young man working at the front counter.
The lot had very few cars and there was nobody in the lobby.
"Evening Albert. Yeah, things should pick up on the weekend," Roger predicted.
He pulled up the reservation that Albert made before he left Utah.
"I'm going to need another room for my friend here," Albert said.
"Hello," Jillian greeted the clerk.
He had known Albert for many years and did not know what to make of his female traveling companion. Albert noted his reaction.
"She is a friend Roger. Now, do you have any vacant rooms or not?" Albert pressed.
Roger gave Jillian another look, before he turned his attention to the computer in front of him.
"Yes, there's one available three doors down from yours."

"We'll take it," Albert said.

After filling out the paperwork and receiving their keys, Jillian and Albert retreated to their room.
"That was a little embarrassing. I'm sorry," Jillian apologized, as they got into the elevator.
They were enroute to the second floor.
"Don't worry about it, kid. You have to learn to not care about what other people think," Albert said.
"I know."

The elevator reached the second floor and they got out.
"They um, usually leave menus in the rooms if you want to order dinner from some of the restaurants around here," Albert suggested.
"I picked up some water and things to snack on at the mall," Jillian said.
"Ok. Well, this place does have the continental breakfast in the morning. Why don't we meet down there by seven," Albert said.
"Sounds good. See you then."
They departed and headed to their rooms.

Chapter 53

After a long hot shower, Jillian pulled on the
flannel nightgown she bought and settled into bed. For
her dinner she chose to have the bag of popcorn and
bottled water also purchased during her shopping spree.
The silence of the room suffocated her as she located the
remote to flip on the television. A rerun of STARSKY
AND HUTCH came on.
"I miss my cats," Jillian said to herself.
To remedy that problem, she turned on her cellphone.
Dante and Anthony's faces popped up on the screen.
She noticed several text messages from Walter, Rosie,
and Barbie.
"Oh Lord, reality. I guess I better start by giving Barbie a
call," she thought.
Jimmy and Barbie had just finished eating dinner.
"Let me get these dogs fed now," Jimmy said, getting up
from the table.
The pack of huskies followed him down to the lower
level of the house where they would be fed.
Barbie had just started to clear the table when her
cellphone rang. It was on the kitchen counter.
"Hello Barb," Jillian said.
Upon hearing Jillian's voice, Barbie flew into panic
mode. She paced about the kitchen as she fired off
questions to her friend.
"Jillian. Oh my God. Where are you? What's going on?
Are you all right?"
"I'm in Lewisburg, Pennsylvania," Jillian announced.

"What? Why?"

In the moments that followed, Jillian updated Barbie with all that had happened to her. She began with her mental breakdown at the Holiday Inn in Riner, to meeting Albert and ending with her decision to accompany him back to Utah.

"Barb, he sort of lives near the Best Friends sanctuary. I'm hoping I can maybe volunteer there or get a job. At any rate, this trip is giving me a chance to find happiness in my miserable life."

It took a few moments for Barbie to digest all the things Jillian had told her. The situation overwhelmed her with disbelief. She never realized how troubled her best friend really was.

"I can't believe it. I really can't believe you just up and took off with a truck driver," she finally said.

"His name is Albert. He's really nice and I trust him. He's kind of like the grandfather I never had," Jillian decided, as she stretched out on the bed in the room.

"I guess," Barbie said, with apprehension.

Jillian sensed the tone of her voice. "Stop worrying."

Barbie decided to change the subject when she asked Jillian if she had quit her job at Lincoln Makes Cents.

"Not quite. I talked to that heifer, Tina, and told her I was going to email Tracy a request for a leave of absence."

"Have you done it yet?"

"I think I will, as soon as I get off the phone with you."

Barbie still could not accept the situation Jillian became involved in.

"Jillian, why don't you stay at that hotel there so that Jimmy and I can come and get you?" she suggested.

Jillian became a little angered by the way Barbie was reacting to her decision.

"No, I don't need the two of you to rescue me. I really appreciate the concern, but I am going to Utah with Albert."

"Are you sure?" Barbie pressed.

"Yes. I just need the two of you take care of my cats, until I can return for them," Jillian replied.

"I went over there around four to feed them and clean the litter box."

"Thank you so much. I will call the Days and tell them I am on vacation and my friends are caring for my cats."

"Ok," Barbie said, sounding fearful.

"Stop worrying Barb. This is something I need to do. I will be fine," Jillian tried to assure her friend.

"I know. Dammit Jill, you call us the minute you need us."

"I will. Bye."

"Bye" Barbie said, close to tears.

She clicked off her phone and drew a heavy sigh.

"James!" she called to her husband.

Chapter 54

After a shower and settling into his hotel room, Albert pulled out his cellphone to call his wife.

"Hello Em," he greeted her.

"Hi Al. How is everything going?" Emma asked. She knew Albert would be calling as she sat up in the living room waiting.

"Jillian took to the road like a trooper. She looks like a kid riding high in that passenger's seat," Albert reported, "You know, like in awe of all she sees."

"That's good to hear. She hasn't had any more crying jags?"

"No. She doesn't eat much either," Albert observed.

"Don't worry. This is all new to her."

"She went right to her room after we checked in. I did give her my cell number if she needed me for anything."

"Well, I am sure she can use a good night's sleep right now and a big breakfast in the morning," Emma assured her husband.

"I hope so. Oh, did you find that tennis racket you wanted to get Joyce for her birthday?"

"Not yet. I think tomorrow's mission will be a trip to Swanson's Sporting Goods in Springdale."

"Or you could shop on the computer like everyone else does," Albert teased his wife.

He loved the fact that she was considered "old school" and had not embraced the use of a computer for everything.

"Oh Albert," she said.

"Well, after I finish off the Italian sub that I ordered for dinner, I am going to bed. Good night."
"Good night. No dozing on the drive." Emma told her husband.

Chapter 55

Tracy's patience for employees not following her office protocols came to an end. As soon as Tina told her about Jillian and her need for a leave of absence, she reacted. The two ladies composed a letter of termination and put together the same packet that was sent to Minnie. It had gone out to be delivered by FEDEX early Friday morning.

"Have you received the request for a leave of absence from Jillian yet?" Tina asked, as she settled into Tracy's office that morning.

The ladies were having their coffee and donuts during their meeting.

"It came to me really late last night," Tracy replied, as she began devouring her chocolate donut.

She was at her desk and Tina sat on the loveseat.

"Did she state why she needed to take it?" Tina asked.

After swallowing two mouthfuls of her treat, Tracy replied.

"Of course not. Here, I made a copy of it for you."

She handed Tina the paper she had printed out earlier that morning of the request.

"The following is a request for a leave of absence from my position at Lincoln Makes Cents," Tina read, "I have a family matter that needs to be taken care of. I am not sure how long I will need. I will keep you informed as to when I will return. Jillian Cole."

"What do you think?" Tracy asked.

"It is pretty short and very vague. I can see why you want
to terminate her."
"Well, she should be receiving the package by noon time
today," Tracy assured her friend.
Tina sat back shaking her head and smiling. It secretly
pleased her that Jillian would no longer be working at
LMC. She finished off her donut.
"Have you questioned Walter or Rosie about this
situation?" she asked.
"I did yesterday. They claimed they had not heard from
her."
"I have my meeting with Rosie at nine this morning.
Would you like me to ask her if she has heard from
Jillian?" Tina asked.
"No. I will go talk to the two of them later. Right now, I
want to compose and send a company email to tell
everyone that Jillian no longer works here."
"Have you decided if you are going to replace her or
divide her clients among other employees?" Tina asked.
"I think I will divide them up between Hillary and
Florence. That should save the company a few dollars,"
Tracy replied.
"And you aren't replacing Minnie either. I should say we
will be saving more than a few dollars," Tina sickly
smiled.
"So, why don't you grab a plastic postal box and help me
clean out Jillian's desk."
"I am here to help you any way I can," Tina said.
The ladies finished off their coffee and donuts, before
heading into the office where Jillian's desk was.

Chapter 56

The theme to HAWAII FIVE O woke Jillian at six o'
clock the next morning. She had set her cell phone to do
so before she finally fell asleep the night before. After
silencing it, she sat up and looked around her hotel room.
"You're not in Riner anymore," she said to herself.
The heavy drapes in the room were still drawn making it
hard for her to see if the sun was rising. After putting on
the lamp next to her bed, she got up.
"It feels so good knowing I don't have to go to work
today."
        It did not take her long to shower and change into
the sweater and jeans she bought. After packing her few
belonging, she straighten the bed and headed down to
meet Albert for breakfast.
        At that early hour, she was the only person in the
dining area. She wasted no time pouring herself a large
cup of coffee and preparing a bagel covered with crème
cheese.
To complete the meal, she took two bananas. Albert still
had not arrived as she took a seat across from the buffet
table.
"I wonder if Tracy responded to my email," she thought,
pulling her cell phone out of her purse.
She pulled up her emails.
        By seven o clock, Albert joined Jillian. He came
to the table with a large glass of milk and a heaping plate
of pancakes.

"Good morning," he said, as he sat across from Jillian.

"Good morning."

She was already on her second cup of coffee. After putting her phone in her purse, she turned her attention to Albert.

Tracy had not responded to her email.

"Did you sleep ok?" Albert asked.

"Yes, I was exhausted."

"And still no regrets about your decision to go West?" Albert pressed, before a drink of his milk.

"Not at all. I um, emailed my boss and asked for a leave of absence. She hasn't responded."

"That was a good idea. It leaves your job open if you decide to return to it."

"Right," Jillian agreed, but sure she would not be doing that. "So, where are we driving today?"

"After we head out of Lewisburg, we will be going through the other half of Pennsylvania, the state of Ohio and into Indiana. If all goes well, we should be spending the night in Elkhart at the Microtel Inn," Albert replied.

Jillian tried to visualize the states they would be traveling through as she finished off her bagel. It did not seem like it could be done in the ten hour frame Albert allowed himself.

"Of course, we will be stopping along the way like we did yesterday afternoon in Pennsylvania," Albert assured her.

"Did you get the weather reports like you did before leaving Massachusetts?" Jillian asked.

"I did. It looks like we might hit some rain in Ohio, but otherwise, nothing to be concerned about."

"I trust you," Jillian said with a smile of appreciation.

Chapter 57

As soon as Albert and Jillian finished their breakfast, they stopped in the restrooms and then headed out to the truck. It did not take them long to get back on the highway to travel towards Indiana.

As Albert predicted, an overcast sky with pouring rain greeted them in Ohio. Jillian felt safe, though, as she watched Albert drive. He kept his speed low and favored the right lane. The traffic around him seem to be adhering to the weather by keeping their speeds down low also.
"In a couple of months, I will be driving in the snow," Albert announced.
"I'll bet that's a challenge," Jillian predicted.
"It can be, but I take it slow or stay off the road until travel conditions improve. You would not believe the accidents I have seen involving big rigs like mine."
"Do the people you work for mind if you opt to stay put in bad weather?" Jillian asked.
"Not a bit. They would rather see me arrive alive, so to speak, than be a six o clock news story about an accident."

Jillian could hardly believe an employer treating an employee that way in regard to traveling in treacherous weather. Tracy lived five minutes away from LMC. The last thing she cared about was her employees welfare during a snowstorm.

"I remember my first winter working at LMC," she began in a trance like state. Her eyes fixated on the wipers.

With each swipe of the blades, she told Albert what had happened.

"A light snow started early on a Monday morning. All of us had made it to the office. By eleven, it had ramped up so much that the mayor declared a state of emergency for the town of Riner. He was closing all public offices by twelve, as well as the schools. He urged everyone else to stay off the roads if they could"

Albert glanced over to witness the distressed expression on Jillian's face.

"Tracy emailed us all and said we could leave at one. She also said to check her weather line to see if the office would be open the next day."

"The weather line?" Albert asked.

"That was a company phone number Tracy used for weather emergencies. She was the one that decided if the office would be open or closed in bad weather. We were responsible for calling it," Jillian explained.

"That tells me she didn't think you folks could judge if you should stay home or not," Albert chuckled.

"Yes, and it was her way of not having to pay us if we did not come in, as it said if the office was opened or closed."

"I see."

"Anyway, I stressed and stayed till one. It took me over two hours to get home. I crawled along Route 495 in my Corolla until I finally made it there."

"I imagine they closed the office the next day, though, right?"

"Not exactly. Her first message on the weather line stated the office was not going to be opened until Wednesday. After roads had been cleared on Tuesday and the state of emergency lifted, she put a message on saying the office would be opening at twelve that day."

"Did anyone show up?"

"Oh, she was there and her sidekick, Tina. I think maybe three other employees were there too. They were the only ones that heard the second message."

"I don't imagine you were one of those three."

"Man, I was home recovering from my drive the day before. Of course, nobody got paid for a snow day."

"Did she pay you people for the time you missed when she let you go home at one?"

"She made them use the PTO time they accumulated. I had none as I had only been working there 60 days."

"That doesn't sound right. The town declared a state of emergency."

"I know, but she claimed employers in the private sector could make their own decisions on how they paid their employees," Jillian replied.

Albert continued at a safe pace along the rain slick highway. He was beginning to understand why Jillian had suffered a breakdown that morning in the parking lot. Working for LMC seem to be a major contributor.

"Looks like folks are behaving and driving slow," he said.

Jillian hardly heard him as she began another horror story that happened on a snowy day.

"We had another snowstorm," she began, "It wasn't as bad as that blizzard, but employees were screwed out of pay for the hours they missed if they did not have PTO hours."

"You don't say."

"It was due to Tracy and her weather line again. This time she left a message saying the office would be open at twelve after everything was plowed out. Well, the plowing was done early, and she left another message saying the office would be open at eleven. Now, nobody heard that second one."

"This is almost sounding comical," Albert observed.

"Oh, it received real laughs when she and Tina gave
every employee a rude phone call asking them where
they were. That included me, too."
Albert rubbed the back of his neck as he sympathized
with the stupidity Jillian had been subjected to.
"Well kid, I take it you have learned from these bad
weather incidents?" he asked.
"Oh yeah. My motto has been "If it is snowing, I won't
be showing". I would just call out and accept a small
paycheck."

Chapter 58

Albert and Jillian arrived at the Microtel Inn located in Elkhart, Indiana that evening. After checking in, they agreed to meet in the lobby to go to dinner. They had chosen to dine at the Cracker Barrel that was in walking distance.

The first thing Jillian did, when she stepped into her room, was check her phone. Earlier in the day, she had received a text from Barbie. Her friend had informed her about the FEDEX packet that was at Jillian's house when Barbie went to feed the cats. Jillian texted her back and told her to take it back to her house. She would call later that night to have Barbie open it.

"Hey Barb, it's Jillian."

She had thrown her duffle bag on the floor and sat on the bed.

"Hello Jillian, where are you?" Barbie asked, as she had just settled down to some television for the evening.

"At the Microtel Inn in Elkhart, Indiana."

"Wow, you're almost halfway across the country," Barbie exclaimed.

"It sure feels like it. So, did you bring the package back to you house?"

"I sure did. Let me go get it."

Barbie headed into the kitchen to take the packet off the island. She then went back into the living room.

"It's from LMC," she said, sitting back on the long, leather couch.

"That can't be good," Jillian remarked.

After setting down her phone, Barbie tore it open and pulled out the contents. The first thing to catch her eye was Tracy's termination letter.

"Barb, are you still there?"

"Ah Jill, the bitch fired you," Barbie slowly said.

"What do you mean?"

"Let me read what she wrote first," Barbie replied, "This letter serves as notice to the termination of your employment at Lincoln Makes Cents. My decision is based on your most recent action of non-compliance to the company guidelines for scheduled leave of absence and the status of your client's insurance ageing. Since…"

"Ok Barb, I have heard enough," Jillian interrupted her friend.

"I'm really sorry."

"Don't be. Besides, Tracy is too stupid to have composed such a thing. I am sure that fat pig Tina did," Jillian assumed, trying to grasp the reality of what had happened.

"Do you want me to read the rest of it?" Barbie asked.

"No."

"Jillian, are you ok?"

It did not take long for mixed emotions to wash over Jillian. Losing a job that she put so much in to over the years hurt. Then she thought about how the toxic work environment drove

her to where she was now. It had caused the biggest part of unhappiness in her life. Knowing that she would never have to go back there made her feel free.

"Yes!" she suddenly yelled, as a huge smile spread across her face.

Barbie did not expect that sort of reaction from her friend.

"Yes, I am ok. Barb, I feel like I've been paroled from Hell."

"That's good to hear. Damn, I wish I could be there with you."

"I know but quit worrying about me."

"Hey, there are some other things in this envelope like info about collecting unemployment, an envelope to mail your office key/ id badge back with no postage and a handwritten check for $72.01. The post it on it says the check is PTO time she owes you."

"I guess that won't be in my last paycheck," Jillian assumed.

"Are you going to call her and tell her you received the letter?" Barbie asked.

"No. I'll just email her."

"Do you want me to send you a picture of the letter?"

"Yeah, it will give me something to smile about on the rest of my trip," Jillian decided.

Chapter 59

Albert retreated to his room. After a trip to the bathroom, he spread out on the bed to call Emma.

"Evening Em, what's going on?" he greeted his wife.

"Hello Al. I'm just watching a little television before bed," she replied.

"I'm here in Elkhart and we're doing good."

"I'm happy to hear that. Is Jillian still enjoying life on the road?" Emma asked.

"Yeah. She really loves seeing all the different places we have been driving through. I don't think she traveled out of Massachusetts much."

"Has she been eating better?" Emma asked, like a concerned mother.

"Oh yes. We're heading over to the Cracker Barrel in a bit for dinner."

"Good. Oh, Connie was over here this afternoon. She told me William was not doing well. They moved him to an ICU room at the hospital," Emma said.

Connie and William Shriver had been next door neighbors of the LaPlante's for over thirty years. They had shared of good times, as well as the bad. Several days ago, William was out in the driveway washing his truck, when he suffered a stroke. Emma had just pulled into her driveway and saw him. Realizing the serious situation before her, she quickly called 911.

"Oh man, that's not good," Albert said, stunned by the bad piece of news.

"I stayed over with Connie for a while tonight and told her to call me if she needed anything."

"That's good. I am sure she appreciated it."

"I'll see what I can do for them tomorrow."

"Well, you keep me posted. I think I better go wash up before I meet Jillian for dinner," Albert decided.

"I understand. I'll talk to you tomorrow."

"Bye dear."

"Bye. No dozing on the drive" Emma ended the call as she always did.

Chapter 60

Tracy spent most of her Saturday morning at LMC. She used the time to catch up on issues she did not resolve during the week. A large coffee and three donuts lay alongside her keyboard as she sat reading a batch of emails from the day before.

"I thought for sure I would have one from Jillian," Tracy said to herself.

She took a few gulps of her coffee and glanced over at the plastic postal tub on the floor next to her desk. It contained all of the things she and Tina removed from Jillian's work area. The item that burned Tracy the most laid on the top.

It was a yellow sign that Tina had designed and hung in each employee's new workstation when LMC relocated several years ago to the new office. Tina had written, "Welcome to Your New Home." Under her greeting, Jillian added her own sarcasm with saying, "Because you're worth it." She had also taped three dimes under it. This represented her disgust over receiving a thirty cent a week pay raise after her yearly review. Tracy resisted the urge to destroy the sign.

"I would love to tear this up and jam it up her ass," she hissed.

After finishing up two donuts and reading her last email, Tracy rolled her chair over to the container of Jillian's belongings. She began to rummage through it and came upon a slim white binder that Jillian had labeled on the spine "CLIENTS." When Tracy opened it, the first thing she saw was an 8 x 10 internet printout of the movie actor, Zac Efron. "Good morning, Grandma" was written

under it. Jillian's coworkers would tease her that she was old enough to be his grandmother.

On the pages that followed, Jillian had printed out photos of all of the television and movie men that she liked. They were preserved in plastic sheets and contained sarcastic remarks about billing and LMC. As Tracy began to read some of them, she grew angry. A comment Jillian wrote under a photo of Josh Holloway said, "Insurance Aging Reports- Like watching paint dry."

The book also contained a picture of Dominic Zamprogna from GENERAL HOSPITAL. Jillian's phrase from him said, "How do I lighten my wallet of $25.00? Lose your office id badge."

It was an office policy that if an employee lost their badge, Tracy charged them $25.00 to replace it.

"I wonder how much time she wasted putting this together?"

She finally slammed the book shut upon seeing the photo of Michael Landon that said, "Suck it up, buttercup."

After throwing it back in the container, she slapped her hand on the desk fully annoyed.

"Getting rid of Jillian Cole was the best thing I have done since getting rid of Minnie."

A gulp of coffee and finishing off another donut helped to ease her anger a little.

Chapter 61

The elation of being "paroled" from LMC stayed with Jillian as she rose the next morning. When she joined Albert for the hotel's continental breakfast at seven, she neglected to tell him though. She decided to save the news until they were on the road to Des Moines, Iowa.

It took them several hours to leave the state of Indiana and cross into Illinois. They were fortunate to be greeted by sunny clear weather as they made their way along I-80W. Jillian continued to be enthusiastic about riding high in Albert's truck and seeing the country. "Did you talk to your wife last night?" she asked Albert. "Yes. She likes to keep me updated on how things are back home," Albert replied, "She did have something upsetting to tell me, though."
"Oh, what was that?"
"Our next door neighbor, Willie Shriver, is not doing well. He suffered a stroke a week ago and they had to move him to an ICU unit yesterday."
"Oh wow, I'm sorry. I know how hard it is to have a good friend hurting," Jillian sympathized, as she thought of Minnie.
"Of course, Emma is helping them out. Man, I hope Willie makes it, "Albert lamented, thinking of his good friend.

Their conversation brought to mind LMC's policy regarding a death in the family. Jillian also thought about how hostile Tracy was if she learned a sympathy card had been sent.

"Do you know that LMC only allowed an employee eight paid hours of bereavement if a spouse, parent or child died?

If you needed any longer than that, you used your PTO or did not get paid," Jillian rambled, "Boy, did I thank God my parents were gone before I took a job there."

"I've had a lot of jobs in my life and all of them allowed at least three days, if not more, and they paid you," Albert recalled.

"Me too. I even held jobs that the employer acknowledged your grief and sent flowers," Jillian added.

"Same has happened to me over the years. It was either flowers or a donation in the person's name, as well as a card."

The mention of a sympathy card brought another disturbing memory to Jillian. She still could not believe such a thing happened.

"Tracy actually lambasted two employees at a staff meeting because they sent around a card for all of us to sign, after another employees father passed away. She intercepted it and tore it up in front of us all. We never knew why she felt this way."

"Incredible. Does she have any family?" Albert asked.

"A husband and two children."

"Not to sound crude, but I wonder how she would react if she lost one of them," Albert noted.

"She's so heartless, it probably would not phase her in the least," Jillian assumed.

Albert glanced over to witness the dark look in Jillian's eyes.

Chapter 62

By midafternoon, Albert pulled off the highway in Genesco Illinois to take a break. They noticed several fast food restaurants in the area and chose to eat at Hardee's.
"I think I need the ladies' room before I order," Jillian said, as she and Albert stepped into the place.
"Go on. I'm heading to the men's room. We can order when we finish."
After Jillian used the facilities and washed her hands, she pulled out her cell phone. The first thing she noticed was a voice mail from Walter.
"Hello Jillian. Where the heck are you? Everyone at the office is worried. Tracy emailed us all to say you no longer work there. Please call me as soon as you can."
Hearing Walter's voice caused Jillian's eyes to well with tears. He was the only person, besides Barbie, Jimmy, and Rosie, that cared about her.
"Miss you too," she said.
She quickly texted him that she was doing all right and would give him a call that night to explain everything.

Chapter 63

Albert and Jillian spent the remainder of Saturday traveling through Illinois and into Iowa. By early evening, they had arrived at the Quality Inn off the highway in Des Moines.
"Are you up to having dinner at the Bonanza Steakhouse? It's in walking distance from the hotel here," Albert asked, as they stepped off the elevator.
They were on their way to their rooms on the second floor.
"Sounds good to me," Jillian replied.
The name of the place made her smile as she thought of Michael Landon.
"Ok. We'll meet in the lobby in about thirty minutes," Albert planned.
Jillian wasted no time calling Walter, the moment she stepped into her room. His phone rang several times as she silently prayed that he would answer it.
"Come on Walter, please be there."
She stretched out on the queen size bed.
"Hello Jillian," Walter greeted her.
Her photo had popped up in his caller id.
"Hi Walter. It is so good to hear from you," Jillian said.
Hearing his voice suddenly caused her to grow misty with tears.
"Are you all right? Where are you? Do you know how much we all miss you?" Walter bombarded her with questions.

"I'm at the Quality Inn in Des Moines, Iowa." Jillian replied.

"What? You're joking. Really, where are you?" Walter said in disbelief.

 He took a sip of the scotch he had poured himself.

"I'm not joking Walter. I'm in Iowa."

He needed another gulp of his drink while trying to comprehend what Jillian had just told him.

"Why? What's going on kid? This is all so unreal."

"Walter, on Thursday morning, I lost it. I mean I really want to just drive to the Cape and jump off the Sagamore Bridge," Jillian began.

"Oh my God, no," he said.

"Yes. I was in my car at the Holiday Inn crying like there was no tomorrow."

"Jill, why didn't you call me?"

"I don't know. I just felt so alone and confused."

"Jillian," Walter whispered, feeling tears come to his eyes. He never imagined that his friend had been experiencing such emotional pain.

"It was there that a truck driver noticed me. He tapped on my window and asked me if I was all right," Jillian continued.

"Do I want to hear what happened next?" Walter asked, needing more of his drink.

"Oh Walter, the man's name is Albert LaPlante and he was like an angel. We shared breakfast at the Holiday Inn."

"How sweet of him," Walter said, with an edge of distrust.

"It was. He just sat there and listened to me unload. I told him how unhappy I was and that my life just sucked. When I finished, he asked me what would make me happy."

"And this led you to taking off with him?" Walter asked.

"In a way it did. I told him caring for animals would make me happy," Jillian replied.

"I don't understand," Walter said.

 "Well, he was on his way back to Utah and I suggested joining him. He lives near the Best Friend animal sanctuary. I am hoping I can volunteer there or maybe even get a job," Jillian planned.

Walter finished off his drink, while trying to digest what Jillian had just told him.

"Walter, we have been on the road for several days now and my anxiety has disappeared. I have not even had the urge to down a bottle of white zin," Jillian said, thinking of all the wine she consumed in the past.

"That's good to hear, but this man, Albert."

"He's old enough to be my father and he's very dedicated to his wife and family. He's also a Mormon, so religion is very important to him too," Jillian explained about her new friend.

 During their long hours on the road, Albert told her about his life. She envied the love and stability that existed within it.

"Ok," Walter sighed, "he sounds like a good man."

"He is. So, stop worrying," Jillian assured him.

"I will try."

"Hey, did you hear the heifer terminated me at LMC?" Jillian asked, hoping to change the subject.

"No. She just emailed all of us to say you no longer worked there," Walter replied.

"She sent me a FEDEX package containing a bunch of stuff. My friend Barbie was at my house feeding the cats when it came. I let her open it last night and she read me the termination letter,"

"Rosie told me Minnie received a package like that too."

"How is Minnie?" Jillian asked.

"Rosie said she is staying in Hawaii until she decides what she wants to do next."

“Good for her. I have got to say, it feels good being paroled from LMC,” Jillian exclaimed.

“We all miss you though.”

“I miss you folks too. Hey, I have to get ready for dinner. Stay in touch,” Jillian said, glancing at the digital clock on the nightstand.

“I will. Bye.”

Chapter 64

Sunday morning Albert and Jillian were back on the road by six o'clock. He wanted to make it to Grand Island, Nebraska in time for the service at the Church of Jesus Christ of Latter Day Saints. He knew Sunday was considered a day of rest in his faith but traveling that week did not allow him to do it. He did know of a place to worship though. Jillian had no objection to his plan and looked forward to attending the sacrament meeting. She knew she had a lot to be thanking the Lord for.

They witnessed the sun rising after finishing off the breakfast sandwiches they had purchased. Without a second thought, Jillian gathered up their wrappers and deposited them in the litter bag pinned to the dashboard.
"Did you talk to Emma last night?" she asked.
Albert took the last sip of his juice and Jillian took the paper cup to throw away.
"Yes. She's holding down the fort," Albert replied, "She told me she already started to do some Christmas shopping."
"Really? It's only the end of September," Jillian noted.
"I know, but my wife does not like to do things last minute."
"Oh no, don't tell me she puts up the Christmas decorations the day after Thanksgiving?" Jillian jokingly asked.
"That's my Emma," Albert chuckled.

The mention of Christmas suddenly caused Jillian to recall all of the terrible ones she suffered through while working at LMC.

"Christmas time at LMC sucked" were the first words to come out of her mouth.

Albert glanced over to see her register that distant and disturbing expression. The pain in her eyes told him bad tales were about to be recalled. He knew letting her talk, though, would make her feel better.

"I can only imagine."

"I remember my first one working there. The day after Thanksgiving, Tracy had a staff meeting to remind us we were not allowed to decorate our work areas or exchange cards and gifts."

"Did she cancel your Christmas bonus too?" Albert asked, switching lanes to pass a slow driver.

"She brought that up too at the meeting. She said our bonus would be a holiday luncheon at some crappy restaurant ten minutes away from the office. She booked it for an afternoon in January, after Christmas."

"So, in reality, the holiday was never celebrated at LMC?"

"Exactly," Jillian agreed.

"It sounds like Tracy might have had a bad experience during the holiday season and was transferring her unhappiness to you folks in the office," Albert surmised.

"I don't know about that, but she did whatever she wanted on Christmas Eve. For instance, one year she went to Disney World and left it up to Tina to let us go home early."

"And what time did she let you leave?"

"Whenever we wanted as long as we had PTO to cover the hours or you would not get paid," Jillian replied.

"That doesn't sound right. My place gives the employees Christmas Eve and Christmas day off with pay. I try to plan my route so that I am home too," Albert said.

"I go in on Christmas Eve just for Hillary's monkey bread and leave by eleven."

"What?" Albert asked, intrigued by the reason.

"Hillary is one of the sweetest people on the planet. Well, every year she makes her loaf of monkey bread and brings it to the office on Christmas Eve. It's a wicked sweet, tasty

treat," Jillian explained, "She knows I like it so much; she lets me have the first piece. Anyway, that's my only reason for going in on Christmas Eve."

The story made Albert laugh and Jillian joined him.

"Well, God bless your friend, Hillary."

"I know. She's one of the best."

"As far as Christmas at LMC, I'm sorry it was so bad. It also makes it another reason to consider a new career," Albert noted.

"Of course."

Jillian had not told Albert about the termination letter yet.

Chapter 65

The praise music had ended. Bishop Williams was beginning his service when Albert and Jillian quietly slipped into the church. It took them a moment to find a place to sit as nearly every pew was filled with worshipers.

"Over here," Albert whispered, leading Jillian to a back seat in the corner.

For the next hour, she sat totally engrossed in the sermon Bishop Williams preached. It revolved around compassion and the need to use it in everyday life. It made her realize it did not exist at LMC. Meeting Albert, though, proved it was going on in the rest of the world. She turned and smiled at him silently grateful for all he had done.

"And we must practice this feeling amongst our families and friends, as well as everyone we meet throughout the day," Bishop Williams said.

Jillian looked around the congregation. Most of the people were families. Husbands and wives, with children, as well as elderly couples holding hands as they listened. She felt a tinge of emptiness knowing that she had nobody. The whole religious outing made her decide things were going to change. If rediscovering the Lord was part of it, she would welcome the opportunity.

Chapter 66

As soon as the service ended, Albert and Jillian stopped at the nearby Panera Bread to pick up a late lunch.
They also used the facilities as it was going to be a four hour drive to Sterling, Colorado. After washing her hands, Jillian checked her cell phone. Her notifications showed that Barbie had called her that morning and, she had Gmail from Tracy.
"I'll call Barbie tonight," she planned, "I wonder what the heifer wants?"
She made the mistake of opening the mail from Tracy.

Jillian: Waiting to hear from you. You left us in a bind with your selfish leave of absence request. People had to put in a lot of extra hours to do your job. Me and Tina cleaned out your desk, so you need to come and get you stuff out of my office. I need your office id/key badge too. I held $25.00 of your pay to cover it for now. Respond asap. Tracy.

Jillian was still feeling the calm peace of mind from attending the church service. Rather than letting Tracy's cruel message anger her, she just turned off her phone.

"I hope Albert remembered to order some warm soup," Jillian said to herself, as she headed out the bathroom door.

Chapter 67

While they drove out of Nebraska, they finished up their lunch. They hardly spoke as the truck rolled down Route 80 to make its way towards Colorado. Years of experience allowed Albert to drive with caution and eat a meal. Jillian sat in her seat taking in the scenery around her.
She had just taken her last spoonful of the soup Albert bought her.
"That was good," she sighed.
"Glad you liked it. Say, what did you think of the church service this morning?" Albert asked.
"I really liked it. I have to confess; I have not been in church since my mom passed away several years ago."
"I understand. People have a lot of things going on in their lives and they neglect the spiritual side of it," Albert said.
"I liked that he was praying about compassion and it made me think about a lot of things."
"I ah, remember you called Tracy a "clueless cow without compassion" during one of our conversations," Albert chuckled.
Jillian slipped into another trance like state as memories of upsetting things she witnessed at LMC suddenly clouded her mind.
"That I did. Tracy never cared about another person's feelings. I remember she fired an older lady we had for a receptionist, because she smelled like cigarette smoke," Jillian conjured up the circumstance.

"She also yelled at my friend Walter for answering a
question from another employee. They wanted to know
how to handle a $3000.00 insurance payment. When
Tracy
heard him helping her, she went off on him in front of
everyone saying management handles that."
"That's just not right. She should have taken the two
employees in her office to deal with them," Albert said.
"I know, but she got a thrill out of embarrassing people in
front of the whole office," Jillian explained.
"Jillian, we've been traveling for a while now and I still
cannot believe you survived working for such a person."
"Another form of embarrassment she enjoyed was giving
a person the "deposit policy violation." This was a pink
sheet of paper listing stupid mistakes done after
submitting a deposit for a client. The violations ranged
from using the wrong size paper clip to forgetting to write
the client's name on the calculator slip. She would check
every mistake off and bring it to the employees attention
at the staff meeting," Jillian explained.
"How many of these slips did you receive?"
"About six of them for paper clip issues," Jillian said,
with a slight laugh.
"I see it never bothered you."
"The first time I got one, it did. Then I thought, life was
too short to let her pettiness bother me."
"Good for you," Albert congratulated his friend.
Jillian took a deep breath while several more
incidents of horror raced through her mind. Albert looked
out of the corner of his eye to witness her expression. He
hoped she would not start crying.
"I think the worst thing she did to an employee was
retract a pay raise given to them."
"What?" Albert asked, in disbelief.
"I told you what a great guy Walter is and how he would
do anything for anyone. Well, Tracy took advantage of

that trait. Not only was he handling his clients, sorting the mail to distribute, and running errands for her, she asked him to train new employees. He agreed to do so and she gave him a thirty cent per hour pay increase.”

“I imagine it was better than nothing.”

“Well, it did not last long. When he became overwhelmed with all the responsibilities, he told her he could not handle the training anymore. She punished him by taking back the stinking thirty cents,” Jillian explained.

Albert listened and further realized why Jillian was in such bad shape when they met in the parking lot of the Holiday Inn. He let out a long breath of air.

“Wow, have you ever wondered why Tracy behaves in the manner that she does?” he asked.

“When I first started working there, I thought about it. You know, maybe a bad childhood or abusive husband made her that way,” Jillian began.

“Yes. Those could be two factors,” Albert agreed.

“Well, I’ve met her husband and he’s a sweetheart. As for her childhood, Tina is probably the only one that knows about that. Conversations about your personal life did not happen with Tracy,” Jillian explained.

“I see. So, what did she say when you told her about your road trip here?” Albert asked.

Jillian suddenly noticed the sun was beginning to set on the horizon before them. As the truck rolled down the highway, the sky took on a grey hue lined with orange streaks running through it. Traffic on the road was light for late Sunday evening. It did not take Albert long to pick up on Jillian’s silence.

“Jillian?” he gently said.

“She fired me.”

“Geez, I’m sorry.” he sighed.

“Thanks.”

"How did you find out?"

"A couple of days ago I was talking to my friend Barbie. She had picked up a FEDEX package from LMC when she was at my house. Later, she opened it and read me the termination letter from Tracy."

Albert could not read Jillian's reaction until he saw the smile spread across her face.

"Are you ok with that?" he cautiously asked.

"Absolutely. It feels like great weights have been lifted off my shoulders. Oh Albert, I really want to thank you for being here too."

Albert reached over to give her arm a fatherly squeeze.

"You are more than welcome. I was really scared for you, but now I am happy to see this adventure has improved your outlook on life."

"It certainly has," Jillian agreed.

Chapter 68

Tina had just made it to the back of the suite heading to her office on Monday morning, when Tracy summoned her. She was sitting behind her cluttered desk ready to begin her workday.

"Good morning Tracy. What did you want?" Tina asked. She walked in and sat herself down on the loveseat.

"I want you to listen to the voice message I got from Jillian."

Tracy leaned over to the phone sitting on her desk. After placing it in speaker mode, she brought up the voicemail from Jillian.

"Hello Tracy, it's Jillian."

"Oh dear," Tina mouthed to Tracy.

"It gets better," Tracy warned her.

"I received your package the other day. I am not going to waste phone minutes talking to you. I'm in Colorado at the moment and will deal with you when I return to Massachusetts. Bye."

Tracy hung up the phone to stop any other messages from being heard. Shaking her round head, she ran her stubby fingers through her short black hair. Then she sat back with a sigh.

"Colorado? What in the world?" Tina asked, taking a sip of the coffee she held.

"I know. Who the hell goes to Colorado?" Tracy snickered.

"I wonder if she has family there?"

"I have no idea. Hell, at least she got my package," Tracy said.

"And she knows that she no longer is employed at LMC," Tina added.

Tracy glanced over at the Jillian's box of belongings still sitting on the floor next to her desk.

"I'm sick of looking at her shit. Will you bring it down to Walter's office? He can look at it since he loves her so much," Tracy sarcastically noted.

"Just let me get my things put away in my office and I will take care of it."

Tina gathered up her purse and coffee, before leaving Tracy's office.

Chapter 69

Walter and Rosie were in their office early that morning. Walter had already begun to sort the mail he picked up earlier and Rosie was texting her friend about their weekend. The position of their desks did not allow them to see if anyone was coming into their office. Melinda's work area was against the wall the door was on, letting her see all that was going on out in the suite. She had not arrived to work yet.

"I got a call from Jillian Saturday night. She said she was in Des Moines, Iowa," Walter said.

"What?" Rosie turned her attention to him, as she rolled her chair almost alongside his.

Neither of them were aware of Tina standing outside listening to their conversation.

"That's how I reacted."

"What is she doing there? Is she ok?" Rosie asked.

Walter relayed to Rosie all Jillian had told him from her mental breakdown at the Holiday Inn to meeting Albert and finishing up with her decision to head to Utah with him.

"I never heard of anything so bizarre," Rosie noted.

"Me neither. I am so scared for that crazy kid."

Tina could hardly wait to tell Tracy what she had heard. At the moment though, she still had to leave Jillian's belongings in Walter's office. She walked right in and placed them beside his desk.

"Good morning."

Walter and Rosie returned the greeting.

"Walter, Tracy wants to keep this box of Jillian's junk in here, until she comes for it," Tina said.

Rosie returned to her desk hoping to avoid conversation with Tina.

"Ok, I have no problem with that," Walter said.

"So, have either of you heard from her?" Tina cautiously asked.

"No, not a word," Rosie quickly replied.

"Me neither," Walter lied.

"Well, she left Tracy a message this morning to say that she is in Colorado," Tina announced.

"Oh, she ah, she probably had things to take care of there," Walter remarked, trying to sound unconcerned.

"Does she have family there?" Tina pressed.

"I don't know."

Rosie kept her back to Tina and Walter averted his glance down to Jillian's box.

"Well, if you do talk to her, she still needs to contact Tracy.

There are a few things that need to be done to finalize her termination from LMC," Tina warned.

"We will," Walter once again lied.

Tina gave him an evil smile before heading over to Tracy's office.

Chapter 70

When Jillian opened her eyes on that Monday morning, it occurred to her that she would be in Utah by the end of the day. She slowly sat up and turned on the lamp next to the bed. The sun had not risen as she looked over to see the digital clock saying it was 5:00.
"I can't believe I actually did this."
She reached for her cell phone and turned it on. Since the start of her journey, she had been pulling up videos of the Best Friends sanctuary. She wanted to familiarize herself better with the facility and decided that Cat World was her favorite. She hesitated to fill out a volunteer application as she was not sure when she would be settled in the area.
"And look at all those babies that need homes," she thought, scrolling through the cats available for adoption.
 "I miss my babies."
She flipped back to her screen saver to see the photo of Dante and Anthony.

An hour later, she was joining Albert for breakfast in the small twenty four hour restaurant located behind the hotel that they stayed in the night before. The two of them chose the endless plate of pancakes and sausages. Jillian knew to keep it down to one cup of coffee, as it would be five hours before a bathroom break in New Castle, Colorado.
"I was chatting with Emma last night. She said she would have a meatloaf dinner waiting for us when we got home tonight," Albert said.

"Are you sure she does not mind me staying in your
house till I can get a hotel room?" Jillian asked.
"Of course not. We have two spare bedrooms upstairs
that have been empty since the children moved out."
"I'm going to have to rent a car too," Jillian planned.
"Well, we can take care of all that tomorrow. Today is
going to be a long one on the road."
"After looking at a map, it looks like we're going to be
seeing a lot of Colorado, as well as Utah," Jillian noted.
"I'm hoping to be in Cedar City by seven this evening."
"Isn't your home in Rockdale?"
"Yes, but I have to leave my rig at the Youngblood Pet
warehouse. I have my truck parked there to drive use
back to my place."
"I see," Jillian said, finishing off a second pancake.
"It's only a twenty minute ride."
"I did the travel calculation from Rockdale to Kanab
where Best Friends is and it is about an hour."
"I never thought about that," Albert said, poking the
sausage with his fork to eat.
"There's a lot of hotels around there too," Jillian added.
"Have you given any thought to what you will do about
things you left in Massachusetts?" Albert asked.
"To be honest with you, I wish I did not have to go
back," Jillian confessed, "but I do have two cats to think
about."
"Um, what about your family and friends?"
"Family. I told you, they live in their own little worlds.
As far as friends go, I will only miss Barbie, Jimmy, and
Walter," Jillian replied.
Albert finished off his last pancake and began to feel sad
for the emptiness in Jillian's life. He still saw hurt in her
large green eyes but hoped a new life in Utah would help
her heal.
"Well, whatever you decide about your living situation in
Utah, you will always have Emma and me to help you."

"Thank you," Jillian sighed.

Chapter 71

By early afternoon, Albert has made his way down Route 76 onto Route 70 in Colorado. He decided to stop in New Castle at a place where they had lunch and he fueled up his truck. While he took care of that, Jillian went into the service station to buy some bottled water. She noticed several editions of local newspapers. Deciding she needed a break from looking at her cellphone, she purchased a few of them to read.

They had been driving for nearly two hours. While Albert concentrated on the road heading to Utah, Jillian perused the pages of her newspapers. She happened to notice a section in one of them that gave small news briefs from cities around the country. A blurb from Massachusetts caught her eye.

It noted that criminal sentencing of Shelly Carmichael for insurance fraud. The lady would be spending twenty years in prison.

"I don't believe it," Jillian said.

"What?"

"This paper has a little piece about a woman from Massachusetts going to jail for medical insurance fraud," Jillian replied.

"I hear that happens quite a bit, like a doctor billing the state's Medicaid agency for services they never provided," Albert noted.

Jillian placed the newspaper on her lap as she looked out the window at the landscape rolling passed

her. Memories of the fraud she witnessed at LMC flooded her
mind. Albert recognized her expression and knew this was going to trigger more bad stories about Jillian's workplace.

"Tracy and Tina were the queens of fraud at LMC," Jillian began, "For example, if an insurance company rejected a claim stating the doctor was not in their network, they would resubmit it with a doctor that was."

"Meaning the doctor, they put on the claim, did not perform the service," Albert reasoned.

"Exactly. They also liked to change the diagnosis codes on rejected claims. You have to be certified in the state of Massachusetts to do that and those two were not."

"Did you partake in their dishonesty?" Albert asked.

"Not a bit. I always refused and never put my name on anything they submitted."

"Good for you, but I don't understand why they were never reported."

"As much as I would have loved to blow the whistle on them, I did not have the energy to collect copies of all the bogus things they did."

"I'm happy to know that you never were involved."

"Thanks," Jillian said, with an assuring nod of her head.

"Were the clients aware of this wrongdoing?" Albert asked.

"I don't think so. They are just concerned with their bills being paid so that they could stay in business."

"I see."

"Each biller kept a daily invoice of the work they did for each client they had. We had to record the amount of claims we sent out, deposits written up and any phone calls or appeals we did. This was sent to the client at the end of the month. I would not be surprised if Tracy or

Tina doctored them up and changed amounts," Jillian continued.

"You never saw the invoice before it was sent to a client?"

"No, she use to have Minnie, our billing supervisor send them out."

"I have to admit Jillian, I have never heard of a place like LMC."

"Well, consider yourself a lucky man," Jillian said.

Chapter 72

By early evening, Albert was making his way down I-15S to the warehouse in Cedar City Utah. Youngblood Pet Supply was located in the first building of the industrial park. When Albert pulled in, the back lot was filled with cars belonging to the workers on the second shift. Overhead lights illuminated the area as he backed his rig into one of the loading docks.
"Now, I can leave her here until they load her up again," Albert said, as he and Jillian made their way inside.
"And you won't be heading out again for a few days, right?" Jillian asked.
"Right. I like to take a few days off to keep my hours of service on the road within regulation."
After taking care of paperwork and a conversation with his supervisor, Albert led Jillian out to the front of the building. This is where he was allowed to leave his truck before heading out on the road. This lot also had sufficient lighting and security cameras.
"It's the black Tundra over there."
He motioned to the vehicle parked at the far end of the building. It did not surprise Jillian to see that he drove an oversized pick up too. After Albert clicked the key to unlock it, he took Jillian's duffle bag and opened her door.
"Climb on in kid."
He threw her bag in the back bed along with his own.

"Wow, after riding high in your other truck, this seems strange," Jillian noted, when Albert crawled into the driver's side.
"I don't think you will see anyone driving without their pants on either," he jokingly said.

Chapter 73

When Albert pulled into the dead end street he lived on, Jillian noticed only two other houses on it. The LaPlante's owned the last one on the left. It was a gray two story Cape with a small swatch of land in the front. In the darkness, she could not make out the rest of the area. He pulled into the driveway behind a small Honda Civic parked in the carport. An outside light shown from the side of the kitchen door.

"Home sweet home," Albert announced.

"It's so cute," Jillian complimented her friend.

"I keep telling Emma, it too much for the two of us, since the kids moved out. She refuses to downsize."

"Albert, I have watched enough of those house hunter shows on HGTV, and the woman always wins the battle of where a couple is going to live."

"I'm not surprised about that. Come on, I'll grab our bags and we can see if that meatloaf dinner is waiting for us."

A sense of peace washed over Jillian when she stepped into the LaPlante's kitchen. The warm smell of home cooking and cinnamon candles clouded the air as soft lighting filled the room. Emma had just taken a pot of boiling potatoes off the stove when they entered.

"Albert, you're home," she greeted her husband.

She was a tall, willowy lady with large brown eyes and short silver hair that delicately framed her face. Dressed in a purple plaid shirt, lightly worn jeans and loafers, Jillian did not expect her to resemble a model from an

L.L Bean catalog. It also surprised her to see the affection between the couple as they shared a hug and a kiss.

"So glad to see you dear," Albert said.

He remembered Jillian was there, as he stepped away from Emma.

"Em, I'd like you to meet Jillian. Jillian, this is my wife, Emma."

Emma reached forward to give Jillian a slight hug.

"Hello Jillian, so nice to finally meet you."

"Thank you. It's nice to meet you."

The ladies stepped back smiling.

"Oh boy, that meatloaf smells good," Albert exclaimed, as he stepped over to open the oven door.

"Well, I do have some potatoes to mash before we can eat it," Emma said, "why don't you take Jillian upstairs so she can see where she will be staying?"

"Sounds like a plan to me. I'll use the bathroom down here to clean up," Albert agreed.

"Thank you so much," is all Jillian could say.

Albert led her down the hall passed the bathroom he would be using and into the living room. Once again, she felt a twinge of envy over the feeling of family that the room conveyed. Orange flames danced in the huge brick fireplace that filled the back wall. A well-worn leather
couch, with a handmade Irish afghan draped over the back of it and loveseat circled the area in front of the hearth.

Around the room, the walls and shelves were filled with family photos and mementoes collected over years of love.

After making their way up the stairs, Albert showed Jillian to the bedroom she would be staying in. "This is it."

He flipped the light switch on. The room had been used by his two sons when they lived there. The walls were

still decorated with Charlie Russell's western paintings and Edmonton Oilers hockey paraphernalia. The bunkbed had been replaced with a king size bed. Jillian liked the white bedspread, covered with silhouettes of black horses, laying
upon it. A nightstand next to the bed was the only other piece of furniture in the room.
Albert noticed her taking in all that the room offered.
"We kept the boy's décor up after they moved out. Only thing Emma replaced was the bed. They used to have bunkbeds."
"It's great. I like it."
"The master bedroom and bathroom at down the hall," Albert said, placing her duffle bag on the bed.
"No master bath in that master bedroom?" Jillian joked.
"Oh no, we roughed it and all shared one bathroom up here," Albert shot back.

Chapter 74

Thirty minutes later, Jillian joined Albert and Emma around the kitchen table for a cozy dinner. Albert recited grace as he thanked the Lord for the meal, a safe trip home and all that was good in his life. He even included a blessing for Jillian. She bit her lip not to cry.
"Ok ladies, dig in."
"It all looks so good," Jillian complimented her hostess.
"Thank you. Oh, did you want a glass of milk?" Emma asked.
She had given Jillian some ice water to drink with her meal.
"Oh, no thank you. The water is fine."
"Em, did I tell you Jillian went to church with me on Sunday?" Albert asked.
"It was a nice experience," Jillian confessed, "I um, told Albert I had a crush on Donny Osmond back in the day. It caused me to do some research on the Mormon religion and I remembered most of what I learned."
Emma found Jillian's revelation amusing as she smiled.
"I told her we lived in Utah all our lives, but we never ran into Donny," Albert added.
"Ah no, we have not," Emma agreed.

As the meal progressed, the conversation flowed very easily. While Jillian gave Emma an idea of her life back in Massachusetts, Emma told her about the LaPlante's life in Utah. Albert had stories to offer also, that he never told on their truck ride across the country.

Jillian could not remember the last time she had enjoyed such a dinner gathering.

With the meal completed, Emma brought out the strawberry shortcake she had prepared for dessert. Jillian accepted a glass of milk, thought she secretly wished for a cup of black coffee.

"Did you get the berries from Gene's Farmstead?" Albert asked.

"Yes. They looked so sweet and juicy," Emma replied.

"This is my favorite dessert," Jillian noted.

"When my mom was alive, she would make a lasagna and strawberry shortcake for my birthday. I never wanted a cake."

"Goodness, our daughter Katherine wanted the same thing on her birthday," Emma exclaimed.

"But she wanted beef stew instead of lasagna," Albert chuckled.

"Well, there's no law saying you have to have cake," Jillian laughed.

"I agree," Emma said.

Jillian was the first to finish her dessert. Wiping her mouth, she glanced around the table and room. She almost wished she could freeze the moment because she felt so good. Albert and Emma continued to finish their treat.

"Wow, this has been one of the best evenings I have had in a long time," Jillian began, "Not only was the meal and dessert great, but sharing time with the two of you makes me forget how bad life has been."

Emma placed her spoon on her plate and gently took Jillian's hand.

"Oh sweetie, it has been lovely having you join us."

"She's right Jillian. Meals are kind of lonely since the kids moved out," Albert confessed.

"I'm sure you thank God that you have each other though. After an evening like tonight, I realized how much I want somebody in my life."

"You're still a young woman and will find someone," Emma assured her.

"I am certainly going to be looking. I think I was so used to being miserable; I closed the door on meeting men and sharing a relationship," Jillian surmised.

"Well, your trip out here gave you a lot of uninterrupted time to think too. It's good to see you discovered another thing that will make you happy," Albert said.

Chapter 75

Jillian opened her eyes the next morning and quickly remembered she had made it to Albert's house. She turned to see the digital clock on the bedstand displaying the time of "5:37". Judging by the silence, she assumed Albert and Emma were still in bed. The drawn curtains made the room dark. Sitting up, she put on the lamp nearby and picked up her cell phone.

"Good morning Barb. It's Jillian."

She knew Barbie would be awake and getting ready to go to work at 7:30.

"Hi Jillian. Where are you?"

"Rockdale, Utah. I'm at Albert's house. We made it here last night," Jillian replied.

"So good to hear you made it," Barbie noted.

"You're not on your way to work, are you?"

"No, not for another half hour."

"How are my cats?" Jillian asked.

"They were fine last night, but they seem so starved for attention, especially Dante," Barbie replied.

"Damn, I feel so guilty. I wish they were here with me."

"I'm sure you do," Barbie sarcastically said.

Jillian picked up on the tone of Barbie's voice and wondered if she was angry.

"You know I really appreciate you taking care of them."

"I know. So, what are you going to do next?" Barbie asked.

Jillian climbed out of bed and walked over to the window.

After drawing the curtain, she looked out to witness the sun slowly rising over a range of mountains. The sight was spectacular.

"Jillian, are you still there?"

"Yes."

She knew her friend would never be impressed by the view that was now taking her breath away.

"How long are you staying in Utah?" Barbie pressed.

"Barbie, I think I want to move here," Jillian quickly decided.

"What?"

"I'll go back to Massachusetts to take care of things and get my cats, but I really think I am going to move out here."

"I see," Barbie choked, "Whatever will make you happy."

The thought of her best friend being so many miles away went beyond being upset. She controlled the urge to cry.

"Barbie, are you ok?"

"I'm just perfect Jillian. Look, I have to get ready for work. I'll take care of your cats. Give me a call when you get back to Massachusetts," Barbie ranted, before pressing the red button on her phone.

"Barbie?" Jillian said, before she realized the call had ended.

She looked out the window once again, as she thought about her friend. She wondered why Barbie's reaction to her wanting to move seemed so harsh. Jillian had expected support and encouragement.

"Geez, should I chalk her up to as one less person that does not give a shit about me?" Jillian puzzled.

Chapter 76

As Walter finished sorting the mail that morning, Rosie sat at her desk posting payments for her client, Dr. Novaris. Sitting by the door, Melinda hammered away on her calculator to tally up the balance of a check deposit. The radio located on the shelf above her played music from the 80's.

"So, I told him to get the hell away from my car or I would break his fingers," Rosie concluded the story she had been telling her coworkers.

Her amusing tale had them laughing out loud.

"You're too much," Melinda said.

"I don't know, Rosie. One of these days," Walter added.

"I know, my big mouth is going to get me in deep trouble," Rosie laughed.

"Are you people working or having a party in here?" Tracy asked, as she suddenly appeared in their office. She made her way over to Walter's desk.

"Please, we'd need some alcohol if we were having a party," Rosie wised off.

Tracy ignored her as she turned her attention to Walter. He could feel her glare as he backed his chair a little away from her.

"Were you looking for the mail?" he asked.

"Eventually, but right I need to know why you did something stupid," Tracy boldly replied.

Sensing the tone of their conversation, Rosie and Melinda kept their backs to the situation and continued with the work that they were doing.

"What are you talking about?" Walter asked.

"I just got off the phone with Dr. Ponce from Blue Rim Eyes," Tracy began.

Blue Rim Eyes was one of the clients that had been assigned to Walter nearly six months ago. The previous biller, Gertie Blake, had been fired after being arrested for

making fake MBTA cards. The Riner police actually took the lady from her desk at LMC and into custody one strange morning.

"I'm still working on some of the accounts that are over ninety days," Walter said.

"And are you writing off large amounts of money without my approval?" Tracy pressed.

"What are you talking about?"

Walter could not believe the accusation, as he knew Tracy or Tina had to approve any write off over $25.00. Before Tracy could answer him, the cell phone in Walter's coat pocket went off. The coat was hanging from the back of his chair.

"I hope you are not going to answer that," Tracy sneered. Walter knew it could not be his mother, as she been instructed to only call his work number.

"No, I'm not. Now, what write off are you talking about?"

Tracy placed a printout she had on Walter's desk. It showed that a $2000.00 charge for a patient named Rita McGowan had been written off. It also showed no follow-up work had been done on it.

"Give me minute to pull this up," Walter said.

He quickly opened the Blue Rim Eye site and entered Rita McGowan's account information. One screen brought up notes on the account. There were none. The next screen allowed Walter to bring up the date of service, as well as the date that the write off occurred.

"February 6th, 2016. Tracy, I was not working this client at the time. If you noticed, the initials on this transaction are GB. That would be Gertie Blake. She used to handle Blue Rim Eyes," Walter explained.

Tracy moved in closer to look at the posting. It killed her to know that Walter was correct in his findings.

"Print that out for me."

Walter made a print of the information and handed it to Tracy.

"Are you going to reverse the transaction that so I can rebill it?" Walter asked, "Or let it go for timely filing?"

"I will take care of it. If you get any calls from Dr. Ponce, direct them to me," Tracy replied.

She left the office and never gave Walter an apology for the ugly episode.

The moment Tracy was out of sight, Walter pulled his phone out of his pocket. He quickly clicked on to see who had called him during the confrontation with Tracy.

"It was Jillian. I'm going out to my car to call her back. Tell the heifer I'm in the men's room if she needs to harass me again."

Chapter 77

As soon as Walter made it to the parking lot, he slipped into his car. He then proceeded to call Jillian back. The phone rang two times before she answered it.
"Hello Walter," she said.
She had still been sitting by the window watching the sun rise and thinking about the previous call from Barbie.
"Jillian, it's so good to hear from you."
"Are you at work?"
"Yes, but I went down to my car to call you back."
"Oh my God, are you sure none of those heifers saw you escape?" Jillian teased.
"After what just happened a few moments ago, I really do not fucking care," Walter hissed.
For Walter to be using profanity, Jillian knew he had to be angry.
"What did they do now?" she asked.
Walter laid out the harsh accusation Tracy threw at him and ended with the fact he was not responsible for the write off.
"But I received the last laugh when I brought up the account myself and saw that Gertie Blake did it. Tracy just stood there like an idiot did not know what to say."
"Gertie Blake. Gee, I wonder if she is still in jail," Jillian said.
"Hmm, that will be something to Google later. Oh, I forgot to mention Tracy never apologized to me," Walter added.
"I am not surprised."

"Let's forget about me. What about you? Where are you?" Walter asked.

"We made it to Rockdale, Utah last night. I'm staying at Albert's house."

"That's good to hear, I think."

"Oh, it is. His wife Emma is the sweetest person and she made an excellent meatloaf dinner and strawberry shortcake. She was happy with me staying at their house too," Jillian raved about her hostess.

"Does that mean you are not coming back to Massachusetts any time soon?"

"Walter, I think I am going to move out here," Jillian confessed.

Her reply caused a wave of unhappiness to wash over Walter. It hurt enough that she had been fired from LMC, but to learn she would be living in another state made it worse.

"Oh Jillian, are you sure?" he pressed.

She knew she would miss him more than she wanted to confess, but a life change was in order now.

She tried to keep the pain out of her voice when she replied, "Yes."

"Do you know how much I am going to miss you?"

"Probably as much as I am going to miss you," Jillian quickly said.

At that moment, she heard the toilet flush down the hall.

To avoid a breakdown on the phone, she decided it would be a good time to end the call.

"Walter, it sounds like Albert or Emma are awake. I think I better go."

"I understand. Keep in touch."

"You know I will. Bye," Jillian said, as she ended the call.

"Bye Jillian," Walter said, as he felt tears welling in his eyes.

“I am going to miss you so much.”

Chapter 78

Walter pulled himself together and returned to his office.
Rosie and Melinda could see the distressed look on his
face as he went to sit at his desk. They turned their
attention to him.
"How is Jillian?" Melinda asked.
"She made it to Utah with Albert, the truck driver,"
Walter replied.
"Wow, I can't believe it," Rosie exclaimed.
"She says she plans on moving out there."
Rosie laid a sympathetic hand on Walter's shoulder. She
knew how much the two of them meant to each other.
"I'm sorry Walter. Geez, I thought she'd just take a trip
out there, clear her head and come back to start things
over here," she said.
"Me too. I guess she was in more pain than we all knew.
I'm just happy she did not do anything to hurt herself
physically," Walter said, remembering Jillian had
entertained thoughts of suicide.
"No kidding. I will bet working here also contributed to
her grief," Rosie predicted.
"Somehow I feel that was a major part of it," Walter
decided.
"Hey, when you were out, I looked at a text I received,"
Rosie said.
"Oh shit, did you break company protocol and look at
your cell phone?" Walter joked.
"Yes, I did. It was from Minnie."
"I didn't see that coming."

"Me neither. She said she's back in Massachusetts and has an appointment to see Tracy at one o' clock today."

"That should be interesting," Walter noted.

"And I will be on the lookout for her," Melinda chimed in.

Her desk faced the open door and allowed her to see all that was going on in the front suite.

"Yeah, we're all going out to give her a good greeting when she arrives," Rosie planned.

"It will show Tracy how much she is missed," Melinda added.

"Well, you can count me in on that party too," Walter said.

Chapter 79

Jillian joined Albert and Emma for breakfast down in the kitchen. As she had slipped into a pair of jeans and sweatshirt, the couple were still in their pajamas and bathrobes. Emma had prepared French toast and bacon. Albert took it upon himself to make fresh squeezed orange juice.

"Good morning dear," Emma said to Jillian.

"Morning," Jillian said, gingerly entering the kitchen. She felt like she should be helping them too.

"Have a seat kid and let me get you some oj. I made it myself," Albert announced.

Emma had placed a large platter of French toast and bacon in the middle of the table, before they all sat.

On that morning, Emma said the grace before the meal. Jillian bowed her head to enjoy the blessing.

"Ok kid, dig in," Albert said, after the prayer ended.

"It all smells so good," Jillian complimented the couple.

"Extra cinnamon is my secret," Emma confessed.

Jillian let out a small sigh of contentment. Once again, being that the table with good people made her happy.

"So kid, what did you want to do today?" Albert asked, helping himself to a second piece of bacon.

The ringing of the telephone interrupted Jillian's reply. The cordless device sat on the counter next to the refrigerator. Emma put down her juice and went over to answer it.

"Hello," she greeted her caller.

"Hi Emma, it's Suzanne."

Suzanne Arthur and her husband, Richard lived two houses away from the LaPlante's. She was William Shriver's daughter. It was a blessing that the families could reside close together. As her parent's aged, Suzanne was able to care for them. Having the LaPlante's nearby proved to be convenient also, as they enjoyed babysitting Suzanne's three children when the Shriver's were not available.

"Suzanne, what's going on?" Emma asked.

"Oh Emma, the hospital just called. My father died. It happened so quickly; the nurses did not have time to notify us before he was gone," Suzanne replied, on the edge of tears.

"Oh dear, I am so sorry. What can I do to help?" Emma asked.

"Richard is up in Salt Lake City for business. Could you come over to get Helen and Paul off to school when they wake up? I need to pick up mom and go to the hospital."

"Albert's home. I'll have him take the two of you to the hospital," Emma decided.

"And Charlie. Oh no, I can't take the baby to the hospital," Suzanne panicked, thinking of her ten month old son.

"Don't you worry I will stay with him. Albert and I will be at your place as soon as we get dressed," Emma assured her.

"Thank you, Emma, thank you so much."

Emma hung up the telephone, before turning her attention to Albert and Jillian.

"Albert, that was Suzanne. Willie passed away this morning," she softly said.

A crestfallen look washed over Albert's face as he thought of losing one of his best friends.

"Oh man, that's too bad," he sighed.

"She needs our help. Richard is out of town."

"Of course. What can we do?" Albert asked.

"I told her you would drive her and Connie to the hospital. I can only imagine how upset they must be."

"I have no problem with that."

"And I'll stay at their house to get the children off to school and take care of baby Charlie," Emma continued.

Jillian could only feel admiration for Albert and Emma. She loved their quick and caring response to the pain that their friends were going through. It made her problems seem trivial.

"Hey, why don't you folks go on to take care of your friends. I can clean up here," she offered.

"Thank you so much," Emma said.

"It's no problem. Do you need anything else taken care of?"

"Not that I can think of."

"Yeah Jillian, you just make yourself at home. We'll take care of things when I get back," Albert said.

"Please, don't worry about me. Go care for your friends."

"Thank you," Emma said.

They headed upstairs to shower and dress, while Jillian cleared the table.

Chapter 80

When Minnie returned to her apartment in Massachusetts on Monday afternoon, a box from LMC was waiting for her. She had opened it to discover Tracy had shipped the contents of Minnie's desk back to her. It was the nasty letter, though, that prompted Minnie to text Tracy. She said she would be in the next day for a meeting.

Word flew around LMC of Minnie's arrival at one o'clock. All of the employees were eager to see her as they really missed her. Every few minutes, somebody would peek out of their office to see if she had arrived.

Tracy glanced at the time displayed in the corner of her computer screen.

"12:58."

She looked over at Tina sitting on the loveseat.

They two of them were in the office together.

"Do you want me to stay here with you when she gets here?" Tina asked.

"No. I can deal with Minnie. She just better return all of the things that are the property of LMC."

At that moment, the security bell rang at the front door. Tracy had a camera overhead that allowed her to see Minnie standing outside from her computer screen.

"It's her," she told Tina.

"I'll go let her in," Tina offered.

She had barely stepped out of Tracy's office when a stampede of employees came rushing up to the front door. Rosie was the first to make it.

"Hey Minnie, come on in," she greeted her friend.
It did not take long for all the other employees to surround her with happy greetings.
"Hello, you guys," Minnie called out.
Walter approached her with a hug.
"I am so sorry for your lose," he softly said, about the passing of Minnie's sister.
"Thank you, Walter. Your card was sweet."
Tina had made it up there in time to hear that comment.
"I'm sure all of you people have work to do," she rudely said.
"And it's lovely to see you again, Tina," Minnie sarcastically sneered.
The employees retreated back to their offices, while Tina faced off with Minnie.
"Tracy is waiting for you. Why don't we go see her."
"I can hardly wait," Minnie shot back.
        Tracy had placed a chair from the lunchroom in front of her desk for Minnie to use.
"Hello Minnie, come on in," she greeted her former employee.
Minnie and Tina exchanged a final glare.
"Have a seat," Tracy said, motioning to the chair.
"Tracy, do you need me for anything?" Tina asked.
"No, we'll be ok and shut the door on your way out."
Tina gave Minnie one more sinister smile, before she closed the door.
        The two ladies glared at each other for a moment not saying a word. They each knew the bitter thoughts racing through their minds were going to cause an explosion of ugly words. Before Tracy could speak, Minnie drew a deep breath and began her tirade.
"Tracy, I am not going to waste my time going on about what a rotten person you are. After reading that nasty letter you put in my belongings, I just want to give you back all your junk."

Minnie had been carrying a cloth shopping bag full of things. She stood and dropped each item on Tracy's desk. "Here is the company laptop, my id/key badge and the stupid flip phone you insisted I carry."

"How nice. Now I can issue a full paycheck to you. I had deleted a few hundred waiting for these items," Tracy said.

"I noticed you did," Minnie said, as she sat back down. "Now, I have a few things for you to sign, as well as the completion of an exit interview."

"No. I have a lawyer friend in Hawaii that told me I did not have to sign anything you give me. As for an exit interview, you would not like my answers," Minnie informed her.

"Oh, really?" Tracy challenged.

"Yes. I imagine you want me to sign something to cover your ass in regard to your overbilling clients or screwing the insurance companies," Minnie predicted.

"Fuck, any proof you had of that has been shredded," Tracy cursed.

"Well, good for you."

"And don't even think about being a whistleblower. Tina is a genius in fixing all things in those departments. Why we even received a thank you from Medicare for correcting our so called mistakes. They love us for our honesty," Tracy prattled on.

Minnie could barely contain the disgust over the human being Tracy was. She wanted to be out of her presence as fast as she could. She got to her feet.

"Don't worry, I don't have the energy or time to see that a piece of garbage like you gets punished. Losing my sister made me realize life is too short."

Tracy let the words sink in but refrained from a verbal war with Minnie. She picked up the phone.
"Tina, could you come see Minnie to the door?"
"I can find my own way out."

Chapter 81

Stopping by Jillian's house to care for the cats had become part of Barbie's routine the past week. On her way to work, she quickly slipped in to give them each a half a can of cat food and fill their water bowl. She also scooped their litter box. Though she hated the task, she knew it had to be done.

Having more time on her way home from work, she stayed a little longer to give them some of the attention they missed. She would sit in the living room where they would crowd around her to be petted.
"Don't worry guys, your mom should be home soon," she consoled the cats.
She spend another twenty minutes with them, before slipping on her coat to head out the door. To prevent them from following her, she placed a handful of treats in their bowls.

Barbie was just about to get into her car when Mrs. Day and Pulaski came into the driveway. The two ladies had gotten to know each other better over the past few days.
"Hello, Mrs. Day."
"Hello Barbie. How are the cats?"
"They miss their mom," Barbie replied.
"I received a call from Jillian today. She made it to Utah," Mrs. Day said.
"She called me too."
"It um, sounds like she going to be moving out there," Mrs. Day gingerly noted.

"I know. I'm not sure, though, when she will be back here to get the cats and her things."
"She didn't tell me that either."
The discussion about Jillian's moving was beginning to upset Barbie. She tried to shrug off the feeling.
"Well, if moving is going to make her happy, I guess it is what she has to do."
"I feel so guilty that I never saw how sad she really was. I wish I could have helped her," Mrs. Day lamented.
"My husband and I felt the same way. She hid it really well."
Pulaski started to get impatient, as he pawed at Mrs. Day's kneecap. He fidgeted a bit and whimpered.
"It sounds like someone wants his dinner," Mrs. Day noted.
"I have to go feed my dogs too. Good night"
"Good night, Barbie."
The ladies departed as the sun began to set in the gray evening sky.

Chapter 82

As soon as the breakfast dishes were finished and stored away the next morning, Albert and Jillian headed out to complete some errands. Emma was already at the Arthur's house taking care of the baby, while Suzanne and her mother, Connie made funeral arrangements for William Shriver.

"Emma is so sweet helping the Arthur's during their bad time," Jillian noted.

As Albert drove, she sat in the passenger's seat of his pick-up truck.

"That's just the kind of lady she is. She told me she felt guilty that she could not help you out today," Albert confessed.

"Oh no, she's done enough letting me stay at your house and making excellent meals," Jillian assured him.

"Don't worry about it," Albert said, "So, where do we need to go first?"

"I think if there is a Walmart or Target around here, I can pick up some of the things I need. For starters, a laptop will make it easier to look for a place to live and job," Jillian replied.

"There's a Walmart in Cedar City. I have to stop at the warehouse over there to see if my route has been planned, so we can kill two birds with one stone," Albert replied.

"You won't be heading out tomorrow?"

"No. The beauty of working independent is I am able to do a delivery route every other Thursday for five days."

"I guess I lucked out last week that you were in Massachusetts when a had a meltdown," Jillian chuckled.

"Have you given any thought as to when you are going back there?"

"Not right now. After I visit Best Friends, I would really like to see what it is like around here. That reminds me, I need to buy a GPS to use while I am driving. The car I rented does not have one," Jillian replied.

"Good idea. When did you plan on going to Best Friends?"

"I want to book one of the tours they offer of the entire place. I haven't done that yet."

"I see."

Albert joined Jillian on her trip into Walmart. While she shopped for a computer and GPS, he headed over to the men's department to look for black socks and a white dress shirt to wear at William Shriver's funeral service. He managed to find both.

"I needed to update my wardrobe for Willy Shriver's funeral," he said to Jillian.

They had met in the front of the store and were standing in the checkout line together.

"Well, I managed to find the two items I needed," Jillian said.

"Do you need any help in paying for them?" Albert asked.

The question caught Jillian off guard. Through their entire trip, she had managed to pay for all she needed. At the moment, she was still able to.

"Oh no. Of course not. Thank you anyway," she stumbled over her reply.

Jillian was the next to capture the cashier's attention.

"And how is your day going?" he asked, with a smile.

The friendly manner seemed strange to Jillian as most from Massachusetts were rude when dealing with the public.

"Good, thank you," she replied, as she placed her items on the counter to be rung in.

Chapter 83

Jillian joined Albert as they made their way into the Youngblood Pet warehouse. Climbing a small flight of stairs brought them to the main level. The facility set up had a row of offices on one side of the hall and the actual warehouse full of product stretched out on the opposite side. A wall of windows enabled a person to see what was going on down below. It also gave the company president the opportunity to watch his people work.
"Ok kid, I'm just heading down to Charlie's office for my schedule. You can hang out here and watch those folks pick and pack pet products," Albert said, motioning to the window.
"It sounds like fun," Jillian chuckled.
He headed down the hall, while she turned her attention to the view down below.

Every corner of the place people were in motion. The back part of the warehouse had twenty rows of shelves filled with everything from cat toys to dogfood. A group of nearly fifteen people walked up and down each aisle pushing what resemble a supermarket cart. The front part held a clipboard with the order, while the cart itself was filled with the items they pulled.

In another corner of the warehouse, more employees handled the process of packing the boxes and sealing them. Then the boxes were placed on skids and wrapped in large plastic sheets to be loaded on the delivery trucks. That area also was used to prepare packages for mail order deliveries.

Jillian noticed the six bay doors open where the vehicles were parked to be loaded. She recalled Albert had backed his truck into one that night they finished their journey.

"Wow, so much going on," she thought.

As she continued to observe the Youngblood employees, she notice the positive interaction they shared.

They seem to be talking, laughing, and helping each other.

One lady could not reach an item on the shelf, a taller man retrieved it for her. Another person had a bag of cinnamon candy that he was going around and offering to his coworkers. Some of the people even saw Jillian in the window and waved at her. All she could do was wave back.

Albert stuffed his travel itinerary in his coat pocket as he made his way down the hallway to Jillian.

"Quite an operation down there, huh?" he said.

"Yeah. I'll be it's more satisfying than working in an office," Jillian predicted.

"Those folks have been working here a lot of years. They work hard and Wally Youngblood knows it. He rewards them well," Albert explained.

"A concept I know nothing about," Jillian mumbled.

They started to make their way out of the building. While doing so, she noticed a bulletin board next to the time clock. It had company announcements and a few job openings. Jillian made a mental note to pull up Youngblood's website and investigate those career opportunities.

The final stop the twosome made that day was to the car rental agency. A blue Toyota Corolla was waiting for Jillian. She had booked it the previous day.

"So, Jillian, do you think you can find your way back to my house?" Albert asked.

They were out in the parking lot. Jillian was sitting in the car. She had opened the GPS and plugged in Albert's address.

"I hope so. I set the GPS to get me there," she replied.

"You're welcome to just follow me."

"I know, but I think I want to take my time and explore the area," Jillian decided.

"Well, you have my phone number if you run into trouble."

"I do. Thank you so much for everything."

"You're welcome. Hey, I'll save you a piece of salmon if you're not back by six," Albert planned.

"I'll be looking forward to it," Jillian said, as she rolled up the window and started the car.

Albert walked back to his truck.

"Dear Lord, please look out for that girl," he silently prayed.

Chapter 84

The day finally arrived for Jillian to take a tour of the sanctuary. She had booked the one that would show her everything that the facility offered to help homeless animals. Albert decided to join her, as he was not due to start a delivery route till the end of the week.
"Wow, it strange being in the passenger's seat," he said. Jillian insisted on driving her rental. She had the GPS set and felt confident they would make it to Kanab.
"You never let Emma drive you around in her Subaru?"
"Nope. It's my Tundra, or she stays home," Albert joked.
In the two hour drive, Jillian found it hard to concentrate on the road. The majestic beauty of the area around her proved to be a distraction. Upon reaching Angel Canyon, this was the first time she had witnessed such a remote desert area. The formation of the red rocks dotted with pine trees and brush lined the horizon. The closer she got to the visitor's building, the more excited she grew.
Albert sensed her elation.
"I don't know Jillian, are you sure you don't want me to take the wheel?" he asked.
"N-No, of course not," she stammered, slightly embarrassed.
"Ok"
"I ah, I just want to savor this feeling."
He gave her shoulder an encouraging squeeze, as she smiled at him. Not only did it feel great to finally reach

her goal, but it also felt even better to have a friend like Albert.

They continued into the visitor's parking lot where Jillian parked the car. She wasted no time getting out and using her cellphone to snap a picture of the building in front of them.

"Guess where I am," she texted to Barbie.

Albert got out of the car and walked up to her.

"Is a selfie going to be next?" he asked.

"That's not my style. Come on, let's go inside," Jillian replied.

Several people were milling around the lobby, as they made their way up to the clerk at the front desk.

"Good morning folks," he greeted them.

"Good morning. I'm Jillian Cole and I want to help save them all."

EPILOGUE

In the months that followed, Jillian relocated to Utah with her cats. Her outlook on life improved as she found happiness in working as a packer at Youngblood Pet Products and volunteering. Two times a month she spent in Cat Town at Best Friends and four times a week she was helping out at the shelter in her new hometown of Rockdale.

The LaPlante's remained closely in Jillian's life by a weird twist of fate. Richard and Suzanne Arthur had purchased the vacant land on the other side of Grant Street to build a large home for their family. This allowed Jillian the opportunity to buy the small Cape they were living in. She had gained a whole new circle of friends that included the LaPlante's, the Arthur's and Connie Shriver. She did continue to keep in touch with Barbie and Jimmy. Despite all the changes, she could not bring herself to convert to the Mormon religion. Coffee and wine meant too much to her.

Minnie Shepard returned to Hawaii to live. After earning a certified nursing assistant certificate, she landed a job at the assisted living facility her sister, Andria used to manage. She really enjoyed her new career and the people involved. Her only regret was that that she wished she had gotten into the field at a younger age.

Through the influence of social media, Lincoln Makes Cents went into bankruptcy and eventually closed. Nearly every employee that worked there at the time Minnie and Jillian did, had left. When Tracy posted an open position on the INDEED website, the list of negative reviews that went along with it, acted as a deterrence for people to apply. The lack of employees meant that work did not get done. In a matter of time, the clients either found another agency or did the billing in their own offices.

Not quite old enough for retirement or financially stable, Tracy and Tine were forced to be the employee not the employer.

When Rosie left LMC, she found a job in the billing department of a large hospital in Boston. Walter decided to retire. After his mother died, he bought an RV. He had saved enough to travel all over the country with his cats.
The first place he drove to was Rockdale, Utah.

About the Author

Ellen Grasso now lives in a small town in southwestern
Virginia. With two dogs and two cats, she still has time to
write. Having completed LUNCHBREAK,
PERCENTAGE and CONSEQUENCES BE DAMNED,
she has already begun her fourth novel called A
MILLION FOR ONE.
She has also left the medical billing profession to work in
a more rewarding career as a certified nursing assistant.
The BEST FRIENDS animal sanctuary is another passion
in her life. For many years she has been donating to their
cause and rallying for their goal of an entire country full
of no kill animal shelters by 2025.